FELICITY GREEN

Witchy Muse & Ghostly Clues

A SCOTTISH WITCHES MYSTERY

Cover Design by CoverAffairs.com

Print ISBN: 978-3-911238-06-9

CHAPTER ONE

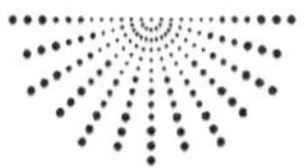

"I, Alexander Malcom, take you, Bethany Anne, to be my lawfully wedded wife…" The handsome man in front of me repeated the reverend's words.

I tried not to be intimidated by the magnificent church and the many rows of Scotland's upper crust in designer gowns and tailored suits. I only wanted to focus on Alexander.

Looking into his moss-green eyes, I felt myself recenter.

My heart beat like crazy when he continued, "To love and honor you, for better or for worse, for richer or for poorer…"

I couldn't foresee any bad days with this wonderful man. And we wouldn't have to worry about poverty either. Alexander was a famous artist, but he also had family money—he was the owner of a castle! A huge, impressive castle that would be my home from now on.

I had to restrain myself from brushing back the unruly strand of dark hair across his forehead and instead held out my hand so he could slip the ring onto my finger. "With this ring I thee wed. With this body I thee worship…"

Oh, that body! It was the strong, muscular body of a

Scottish Highland warrior, but Alex had the tender touch of a sculptor. His large hands were as gifted in discovering the most subtle beautiful lines in a block of limestone as in teasing pleasure out of me.

I felt heat rising to my cheeks and saw a flicker of bemused understanding in Alex's eyes. He knew me so well, despite our brief courtship. We were soul mates.

When the reverend pronounced us husband and wife, Alexander inched closer, careful not to step on the hem of my intricately embroidered designer wedding dress.

"You may now kiss the…"

Ding, ding, ding, ding, ding!

I jumped, hitting my head against something hard.

"Ladies and gentlemen, we have begun our descent into Glasgow. Please return your seat to an upright position and fasten your seat belt..."

Confused, I rubbed my sore skull. My hair was a tangled mess, escaping from its bun. It had nothing in common with the elaborate up-do I had admired earlier in the mirror.

I slowly but surely caught on to the fact that it had, regrettably, just been a dream.

I had an unpleasant taste in my mouth and grabbed the water bottle from the seat pocket. There was drool on my chin, and I surreptitiously wiped it away.

I could count myself lucky that Alexander Malcom Campbell was nowhere near me in my current state. The chances of him falling head over heels for me were slim.

Before I could do anything about my appearance, the elderly lady next to me gave me a nudge and pointed at the seat belt sign.

Sighing, I dug around for the seat belt in my cramped seat. It was no wonder I'd bumped my head against the sloping roof above the window. When I'd requested the window seat, I hadn't expected to be traveling economy.

Alexander might be incredibly wealthy, but there was no reason for him to spoil me. I was only his employee, after all, and not his wife.

Yet.

I pulled the elastic out to redo my hair. That's when I noticed how pale my seat neighbor looked.

"Are you okay?" I asked.

"I've never enjoyed flying much." The lady sitting next to me seemed to be grandmother's age, and she gave me a nervous smile.

I'd never been on a plane before, but I'd been too distracted with fantasies about my new employer to let myself get anxious. Maybe a distraction would work for this lady too.

"I'm Bethany Prince," I introduced myself.

"Adele Martenson. Pleased to meet you."

"What brings you to Scotland?"

"I'm visiting an old friend. How about you?"

"Work. My first job, actually. I just graduated from Boston University with an art history degree." I couldn't help but sound a little proud.

"How exciting! Well, it makes sense you're looking for work experience in Europe, then. Where will you be working? A museum?"

Adele already looked much more relaxed, so I decided to open up.

If she was anything like my parents, she might not approve of what I was doing. But since I'd never see her again, it didn't really matter.

I pulled my purse out from under the seat in front of me and took out the envelope that contained my travel documents, the job advertisement I'd cut out from the magazine, and the pictures Alexander had sent me.

"I was looking for a job at an auction house or something like that. I love antiques and wrote my thesis on furniture makers in the UK. But I couldn't find anything suitable, and then I saw this ad."

I showed it to Adele.

"Muse wanted," she read aloud. "Renowned Scottish sculptor seeks muse for artistic inspiration in exchange for small salary and room and board on an estate in Scotland. Must understand and appreciate art. Travel expenses will be covered."

Adele's pale blue eyes glittered. "How interesting."

"I thought so too!" Encouraged by her enthusiastic reaction, I took out the photos. "I felt compelled to apply. Obviously, I applied for other jobs too," I babbled on, my parents' objections still in my ear. "But I soon got an invitation for an interview via video chat. I spoke to the artist himself, and of course I'd looked him up before. He was very interested in my studies and my thesis. It was all very serious. I know it seems unconventional, but I really think being this sculptor's muse will give me a chance to get to know the smaller Scottish art scene. You know, to network and stuff."

It wouldn't help me find a job in the field I was really interested in, but it sounded good. That was what I'd told my parents and Alexander, so I thought it would also convince Adele.

I couldn't fool her, though.

"What an adventure, to be so close to a famous artist!" she swooned.

I began to nod vigorously but stopped when she continued.

"I used to live in a commune. There was this artist who liked to draw me in the nude. I was always keen to inspire him, if you know what I mean." She winked at me.

"Oh, no… I mean, I'm sure it's not like that…" I sputtered. Heat rose to my cheeks. Of course, my friends had made crude jokes along the lines of what Adele was suggesting, but I was certain Alexander had very honorable intentions. I kept my own romantic ideas to myself, though they admittedly weren't altogether that far off from what Adele imagined.

I showed her the photos. "Look. He sent me these pictures."

There were professional black-and-white shots of his sculptures and also snapshots of the property he owned.

"This is a real Scottish castle!" Adele exclaimed.

"I know!" It came out loud and squeaky. "And that's where I'll live with the artist. Isn't that amazing?"

"What's this?" Adele held up a picture of a tiny, run-down cottage.

I shrugged. "Just a building on the estate. Maybe the estate manager lives there." I took the pictures from Adele's hands and stuffed them back into the envelope.

Just then, the plane touched down on the runway. Adele flinched, and I grabbed her hand.

"Everything's okay." I smiled encouragingly. "We made it."

She exhaled with relief. "Thank you, dear. For chatting with me and taking my mind off the landing." Adele clearly saw right through me.

"I wish you all the best of luck. Such an exciting time ahead of you! A wealthy Scottish aristocrat and famous artist. You, his muse, who inspires him to greatness." She squeezed my hand. "This story is bound to have a fairy-tale ending, dear."

"I know! I hope so too," I answered with a grin. "It feels like a dream."

The unfortunate thing about dreams is that they rarely have a lot in common with reality.

CHAPTER TWO

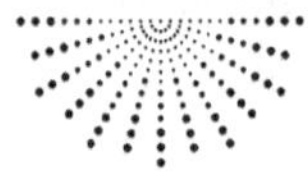

Sometimes dreams just cannot measure up to reality; they turn into nightmares.

I should have known something was wrong the moment I walked through Arrivals.

I'd taken my time fixing my appearance in a restroom in the airport terminal. I'd changed into the fresh shirt I'd put in my purse, straightened my unruly long auburn hair with a flat iron, and reapplied my make-up.

On my way through Duty Free, I'd given in to the temptation to buy a new perfume that, according to the advertisement, smelled like a warm summer night. What's more romantic than warm summer nights? In any case, it had to smell better than me after ten hours on a plane, so I'd doused myself with it right there and then.

When I'd finally gotten to the baggage claim, my huge pink suitcase had been the only one doing its rounds on the carousel.

I'd unzipped it to change into the sexy black sandals that hadn't fit in my purse and stuffed my sneakers into the suitcase.

By the time I made it out of the airport, I was worried about being late.

I hadn't expected that Alexander would pick me up himself, of course. I was looking for a chauffeur in uniform and with a black cap, holding up a sign with my name on it. But I couldn't spot him.

So I was standing there, a little lost, with my pink suitcase, watching arrivals from another plane greet their family and friends enthusiastically.

Near the door, I spotted a grubby-looking older man with a cell phone to his ear. He was scratching his crotch with his other hand, but he had a dingy bit of cardboard under his arm. There was illegible handwriting on it… I thought I made out a P and an R.

I approached him hesitantly. Surely this couldn't be my ride, could it?

The man caught my gaze and looked me up and down.

"Naw worries, aw think aw founder." He put the phone away. "Prince?" he asked me.

I just nodded.

"Yar took yar time. Yar lucky aw waited."

He disappeared through the door without making sure I followed him, let alone offering to help with my heavy suitcase.

Luckily, his car—an ordinary cab—was parked just outside.

I dropped the suitcase next to the trunk with an "oof" and demonstratively crossed my arms in front of my chest.

He seemed to take the hint and put the suitcase in the car for me.

"Blimey, what are ye carrying in there? Bricks?"

Since I wasn't sure if that's what he actually said in his strong Scottish accent, I didn't reply.

I just got into the back of the car.

It smelled of stale cigarette smoke and fake eucalyptus from the three trees dangling from the mirror.

I groaned. The journey from Glasgow to Oban took over two hours. At the end of it, I'd smell more like tobacco and Vicks VapoRub than a balmy summer night.

I discreetly tried to spray some of my perfume, but that seemed to make it worse.

That's why I wasn't even angry when the cab driver let me out just inside the gate of the estate, rather than driving me to the castle.

It would give me a chance to air out before meeting Alexander.

I was outside the small cottage I'd seen in one photo. Now I realized it had to be the gatekeeper's lodge. My assumption that the estate manager lived here was probably spot-on.

Maybe he was supposed to take me up to the castle.

But nobody was here to greet me.

I rang the doorbell, knocked, and rang again. I left my suitcase where the cab driver had dumped it on the gravel path and walked around the cottage, through a gate, into an overgrown garden. The grass went up to my knees and scratched unpleasantly against my bare skin. Maybe I should have worn tights under my short flouncy yellow skirt, but it was summer, and my legs were one of my best assets.

Changing into high heels earlier clearly had been a mistake, however. I struggled across the wilderness and almost fell. Just in time, I grabbed the ledge of a window. I glimpsed what appeared to be a small, very old-fashioned kitchen. In fact, it looked like something from one of those living history museums. I couldn't believe anyone actually lived in this cottage. The state of the garden confirmed that.

I was about to turn around when I heard a noise.

Holding on to the wall, I took a few more steps in the direction the sound was coming from.

That's when I noticed a large shed behind the cottage. It was actually almost as big as the cottage itself, but it had been hidden from view by big trees.

I wanted to knock, but the sound of loud machinery would have drowned that out anyway, so I just opened the door and stepped in.

I immediately stopped in my tracks.

The shed, which I now realized was a workshop, was flooded with light from the large skylight installed in the roof.

It was like a stage spotlight illuminating the most perfect male body I'd ever seen.

Nope, it wasn't a statue.

It was a real flesh-and-blood man.

He had taken his shirt off, putting his muscular back on display. Since he was holding some kind of tool—which was making the loud noise—his biceps were nicely flexed too.

Even though the lower part of his body was clothed in an ordinary pair of jeans, they were tight enough to show what I could only describe as the type of cute tush you want to bite into.

The thought made me laugh out loud.

At that moment, the noise stopped, and my laughter rang out loudly through the workshop.

The man turned around, and I clapped my hand over my mouth.

The black curls, the moss-green eyes, the serious facial expression: It was Alexander Malcom Campbell himself who was standing there.

Of course; this had to be the artist's workshop.

The finished sculptures and blocks of stones surrounding me should have clued me in earlier.

"Uh...I knocked...but..." I mumbled.

"Miss Prince, I presume?" Alexander gave me a polite smile. "Apologies. I must have lost track of time. That happens when I'm absorbed in my work. Anyway, welcome."

I stumbled forward to shake the hand he stretched out to me. "Bethany."

"Call me Alex."

I almost fell, but Alex steadied me in time. His brows furrowed when he saw my shoes, but he said nothing.

Bowled over by how much his large hands looked like the ones in my dream, I must have held on to him a little too long because it got awkward.

"Umm...why don't we go inside for a cup of tea," Alex suggested, almost shoving me off. He grabbed his T-shirt from a chair and pulled it on.

"Sure. That'll be nice."

I turned to go out the door I'd come in from, but Alex said, "Wait, we can go through here, directly into the cottage."

"The cottage?"

But he was already through another door.

I followed him. "Um, my suitcase is out front."

He nodded but didn't go straight through the narrow hallway to the front door. Instead, he turned into a room that I recognized as the old-fashioned kitchen I'd seen through the window.

"Have a seat." Alex pointed at a large wooden table with a bench and several chairs that took up most of the kitchen.

There wasn't a counter like in every kitchen I'd ever been in, only an old Welsh dresser with blue paint peeling off, a stainless steel sink, and a very old wood-fire stove. The most modern item in the room was the fridge, which looked like it was from the fifties.

Alex filled an iron kettle with water, then put it on the stove. He opened the door, stirred the ashes, and added a piece of wood.

I would have much preferred tea in the castle, but I didn't want to be rude. So I carefully perched on the edge of the corner bench. The floral-patterned seat cushions looked a little dingy, and I didn't want to touch them with my bare legs.

Again, I regretted my outfit choice. I hadn't seen a car, so it was possible we'd have to walk to the castle. My shoes definitely weren't suitable for that.

When Alex offered to bring in my suitcase, I nodded with relief. "I think I'd better change my footwear." I smiled ruefully.

But when he came back a moment later, he was empty-handed. I looked at him questioningly.

"I put your suitcase in your room."

For a moment, I thought I'd misheard him. "Excuse me?"

"I put it in your room. It's the first door on the right." He turned his back to me to get a teapot and cups and saucers down from the Welsh dresser.

Stunned, I just looked on as Alex prepared the tea. He had to be joking, right? But there was no twinkle of amusement in his eyes whatsoever. He looked dead serious.

He even frowned when he saw my reaction.

"Is something the matter?"

"It's just…my room is…here? In this cottage?"

Alex raised an eyebrow. "Where else would it be? Do you take milk and sugar?"

"Um… Milk, no sugar, thanks." I swallowed. "I…I guess I thought I would stay at the castle."

Alex laughed. Ordinarily, I would have taken pleasure in the way the corners of his eyes crinkled, but I was a little offended.

"Sure, you can stay there if you want the haunted castle experience. But trust me, you'll be a lot more comfortable here."

I looked around the kitchen in dismay. More comfortable here?

"What do you mean, haunted castle experience?"

Alex gave me a scrutinizing look, the bottle of milk still in his hand.

"I thought you were joking. Did you really think you were going to stay in the castle?"

He sat down in a chair.

My initial anger at his dismissive laugh turned into humiliation. I tried not to cry.

I didn't quite know what he was saying. I could only guess that he invited guests to stay at his home for a Scottish castle experience, but since I was his employee and not a guest, I didn't qualify for that.

I was only here to assist him in his work as an artist.

My romantic dreams burst like soap bubbles.

I bravely stuck out my chin. "Of course. I understand. I can make do with this. They don't call it starving artists for nothing, do they? And that's why I'm here, after all. For the art."

"O…kay." Alex seemed confused.

I stood up, this time with a genuine smile. I'd always had a knack for making lemonade out of lemons. Of course, I'd have to go through a few obstacles before Alex fell madly in love with me. Every rom-com had taught me that. And if I thought about it, this was even more romantic. I'd have to swear off my materialistic worldview and learn to live off art, ideals, and love alone.

"I'm just going to freshen up before we have tea. Is there a bathroom?" I'd seen a pig trough in the garden, and I'd make do if I had to wash there. I had been camping before, and this couldn't be any worse.

Again, Alex gave me a funny look. "Of course there's a bathroom. It's right opposite your room."

I nodded with relief and then stalked out of the kitchen with my head held high—and this time without stumbling on my heels.

If this was a test of the strength of my character, I intended to pass it with flying colors.

CHAPTER THREE

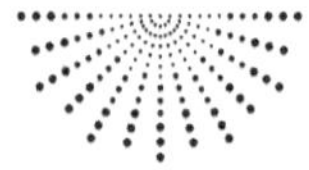

"Your tea might be cold by now." Alex looked up from the newspaper he had been reading when I came back into the kitchen, freshly showered and wearing a new outfit.

"That doesn't matter. I'll just make myself a new pot," I said and bravely reached for the heavy kettle and filled it up with water.

Then I hesitated in front of the stove. There were no plates or markings like on the induction cooktop at home. Did you just put the kettle anywhere on the iron plate?

"You're probably starving after the long flight." Alex interrupted my thoughts. I pursed my lips and nodded cautiously. "There's a stew in the big pot in the fridge. It just needs reheating."

I breathed a sigh of relief. So the cook from the castle would provide for me after all. I would hate to admit that my culinary skills were restricted to fried eggs and pasta. There seemed to be no oven I could pop a frozen pizza or ready-made meal into.

Or maybe this steel contraption had oven capabilities? I unceremoniously dumped the kettle on the stovetop and bent down to fiddle with what looked like an oven door.

Alex came over and opened the oven for me. It was the compartment with the fire. "It's all right. You don't need to put another log in yet."

Then he must have seen my face because he followed up with. "I suppose you're used to more modern kitchen appliances."

"Yes," I admitted.

Alex got the pot of stew out of the fridge and put in on the stove, showing me where to place it.

"Thanks," I said with what I hoped was a relaxed smile. "I'll be fine. You can go if you like. Do you want me to be at the workshop at a certain time tomorrow?"

Alex looked at me in surprise. "This'll be my supper too. I thought we'd eat together. Unless you insist…"

"No, no," I interrupted him hastily. "I just thought you would…um, I mean, I'd love to eat together!"

Now my smile was genuine. Alex was already ready to loosen the strict employer-employee boundaries he'd set. That was encouraging.

"Well, it would have been difficult if you had insisted on eating your meals alone," Alex said with an amused tone as he set the table. "Where would I go? Hide in my room or the workshop?"

"Oh, no, I just thought you were going back to the castle to eat, that's all." I stirred the bubbling stew, then turned around to see Alex staring at me.

"Back to the castle? Why would I…" A sudden realization passed across his face. "Oh, I think there's been a misunderstanding. You must have gotten the impression that I live in the castle. No, Bethany, nobody lives there. This is my home."

Now it was my turn to look confused. "This…little old cottage?" I caught myself before describing it in more unflattering words. "But why would you…I mean…you own the castle, don't you? You're rich! There's no reason—"

Alex laughed.

I winced and shut up.

"It's not just me who owns the estate—it belongs to my family. I'm certainly not rich. I count myself lucky that I can live here for free in exchange for managing the estate. I couldn't even afford the rent for this…what'd you call it? Little old cottage."

I stared at him with my mouth agape. An awkward silence stretched for too long.

The amusement in Alex's eyes slowly disappeared. "What did you expect?"

My knees felt a little weak. I made it to the kitchen bench and sank down on it. "Well, I thought you were a successful and wealthy artist. That's the impression you gave me," I added, a little defensively.

Alex sat down opposite me. "I'm sorry you got that impression, Bethany, but I never said anything that implied that."

"Oh, please! You called yourself a renowned artist in the ad! You sent me pictures of your castle. And you hired a muse from across the world, flying her over… What was I supposed to think?"

"I am a renowned artist," Alex replied in an icy tone. "My sculptures have won some major awards. That doesn't make my work profitable. I've worked hard over the past year, and yet I'm very unhappy with the results. My Aunt Mary, who is my patron, thinks I lack inspiration. She had the idea about a muse and placed the ad. She watched the recorded Skype interviews and chose you. My aunt paid for your travel expenses and also your salary. And I sent you photos of this cottage. The workshop, the cottage, and *one* photo of the castle." He leaned back in his chair and crossed his arms in front of his chest. "Is that the reason you're here? Because you thought I'm a wealthy castle owner?"

"No!" I swallowed. "That's not *the* reason. I'm here because I want to gain work experience. I thought it was exciting and different, compared to the usual unpaid internships in museums. To be up close and personal with an artist and learn about their creative process. And I thought familiarizing myself with the smaller Scottish art scene was less overwhelming than being a very small fish in the art world of a big European city."

"Oh, I remember now. You gave those same platitudes in the interview." Alex's eyes were sparkling with anger now.

"Those weren't just empty buzzwords," I said indignantly. "That's what I really think." I ran my hand through my hair in frustration. I didn't know how to make it clear to him I was really interested in his art and that my career was important to me, but I still had other hopes and dreams. "My expectations were just a little different, that's all."

"You've made that abundantly obvious. What did you expect? That you'd live like a princess in a castle? Is this…" He made a sweeping gesture. "Not good enough for you?"

"I didn't say that." Now it was me who crossed my arms angrily in front of my chest.

"You didn't need to. Your face says it all."

"Now, wait a minute. I might have expected something different, but when I thought I had to stay here while you were going back to the castle, I didn't complain, did I? I—"

I broke off, sniffing the air. "Something smells funny."

"The stew!" Alex jumped up. He frantically stirred the pot and then grabbed a potholder to carry it to the table. "It's a little burned," he said in a dry voice. "I suppose you don't want to eat it now."

"I don't have a problem with it. I'm not the spoiled princess you obviously think I am."

I stood up gracefully, grabbed the ladle and dished a generous portion onto both our plates.

Alex sat down and looked at me with a raised eyebrow.

I also took a seat, picked up my spoon, and bravely dipped it into the foul-smelling stew.

I met his challenging gaze and put the spoon in my mouth.

It was disgusting. I had no idea what I was eating. Beef and potatoes, I imagined. "Delicious," I said.

Alex also started to eat. Suppressing a grimace, he shoveled the stew in until his plate was empty.

"Would you like something to drink?" he asked. "I don't have champagne or anything you were probably expecting to be served, but let's see what else is in the fridge."

"Beer!" I blurted out. "I'm partial to a nice cold brewsky. If you have one," I added, really hoping he didn't.

"Sure." Alex handed me a cold bottle from the fridge. "Let's toast to a fruitful collaboration. To be completely honest, I didn't know what to expect myself. I wasn't sure about this whole plan. And you clearly had different ideas about the job too. But my aunt is convinced that something good will come out of it. We didn't have a great start, but here's to giving it a try."

I nodded and lifted my bottle to clink with his. "To a successful collaboration."

We finished our beers in silence. I was mostly occupied with trying not to grimace, getting the bitter liquid down my throat.

When Alex said he was knackered and would turn in for the night, I was actually glad.

"I'll just finish my stew," I said. My plate was still half full.

"Would you mind doing the dishes?"

"Oh no, not at all," I said, a little too emphatically. "I love doing dishes."

"Okay… Good night, then."

"Good night."

When I heard his door close, I jumped up in relief. I got a glass from the dresser and held it under the running tap.

Then I gulped it down to get rid of the disgusting taste in my mouth.

I scraped the rest of my stew back into the pot and then did the dishes. After everything was clean, dried, and tidied away, the stew was cool enough to be put back in the fridge. I wouldn't be eating it again tomorrow, but I couldn't just let it spoil in the kitchen, could I?

I spotted a selection of deli meat and small meat pies on the bottom shelf. My stomach growled, and I greedily took a few bites.

My mouth full with delicious pie, I had to giggle.

Thinking about it now, the whole dinner scene had been pretty comical. I could have just admitted that I wanted something else to eat. Alex had already formed his opinion of me, and I might as well be my true self.

This certainly was turning out to be very different from what I had imagined. What was I letting myself in for?

Well, at least I would get a funny anecdote out of it. It would be good to keep a sense of humor if I had to travel home in a few days and listen to my parents say they'd told me so.

CHAPTER FOUR

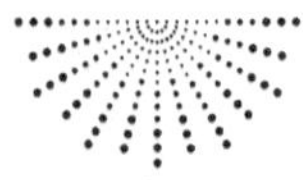

I had the best night's sleep in a long while. It surprised me, since my bedroom was hardly the most comfortable I'd ever slept in. Then there was the jet lag everyone always talked about. Maybe I was immune. And also, I'd been physically and emotionally exhausted.

When I saw how late it was, I jumped out of bed, then carefully opened the door and peeked through the crack. I didn't want Alex to see me with messy hair and no make-up. The coast was clear, so I scurried across the hallway, only to hesitate again in front of the bathroom door. It had no lock, and I certainly didn't want to add the embarrassment of catching Alex on the toilet to our already complicated relationship.

Then I heard a soft clatter from the kitchen, so I quickly went into the bathroom and got ready. Twenty minutes later, I was happy with my natural-looking make-up and wavy auburn locks.

Back in my room, I was faced with the difficulty of finding an appropriate outfit.

My suitcase was chock full of clothes, but I had chosen them with a "dress to impress" mindset, and everything that had looked impressive in the US seemed completely wrong in this cottage.

Alex already thought I was a spoiled princess, so impractical, frilly dresses were out of the question.

In the end, I opted for a simple fifties-style summer dress with spaghetti straps and a sweetheart neckline. The hemline went past my knees, and the cornflower-blue fabric looked great in contrast with my hair, which I restyled into a high ponytail.

When I finally made it into the kitchen, there was a hearty breakfast on the table.

The smell of bacon made my mouth water.

"Good morning," I said, plunking myself down in front of the platter with thick slices of bacon.

"Good morning. Can I get you tea or coffee?" Alex asked. He was at the stove, probably waiting for the kettle to boil.

"Coffee, if you have any?"

Alex pointed at the cafetière and a bag of ground coffee on the table.

I spooned a generous amount of grounds into it, and Alex filled it up with hot water.

"Thanks."

"All right, help yourself."

I tried to restrain myself, but everything looked so good. "What's that?"

"Tattie scones," Alex answered. "Potato cakes."

I sampled one of the triangular flat pieces, and it was delicious.

Alex and I managed to be very civilized, making small talk over breakfast, and things were looking up.

Once we'd cleared the table and the dishes were washed and stashed away, things became awkward again.

"I should really get to work," Alex said.

"I guess that means me too." My voice was a little

squeaky. When he said nothing, I followed up with, "What did you have in mind? I mean, what exactly should I do, as your muse?"

Alex chewed on his lower lip. "I don't really know. Like I said, my aunt was the one who came up with this idea. I guess…you could be my model. I could make some sketches. Maybe that'll spark a creative idea."

"All right," I said with enthusiasm. That didn't sound too hard. I just had to sit there and look pretty.

Alex carried two chairs and an easel into the garden and set everything up. Then he asked me to sit down.

He studied me with such an intensity that I felt my cheeks blush. I had to look away.

"Undo your ponytail, please."

I did as he asked and let my wavy hair cascade over my shoulders.

He nodded and smiled. "Much better."

I breathed a sigh of relief. For the first time, I was getting the impression that Alex actually liked the look of me…which, to me, meant that he liked me.

I hadn't been so sure of that so far.

My confidence came back, and I gave my artist a radiant smile.

"Less teeth, please," Alex said. "I'm half blind. The way you Americans bleach your teeth is insane. Teeth aren't meant to look that white."

My smile faltered.

My good mood only deteriorated from there, as Alex kept giving me instructions. He didn't seem very pleased with how I responded to them. And it wasn't easy to sit still in unnatural positions with all the insects buzzing around me.

Alex also got grumpier by the minute, and unlike me, he did not hide his feelings whatsoever.

He kept crossing out sketches, tearing off paper, and

crumpling it up. It soon became apparent that I wasn't a source of inspiration, but rather frustration, to him.

I slid back and forth on my chair, which was getting uncomfortable.

Finally, Alex pushed the easel aside. "Sorry, but this isn't working. These are nothing but pretty drawings of a pretty girl. Boring. I can't make art out of this!"

I blinked and stood up slowly. My smile was forced, but I put it on nonetheless.

Ever since getting this job, I had been anxious and insecure about a couple of things, but my looks weren't one of them. I knew I was pretty. And I had been sure that was my best qualification for this job.

Before I could say anything in my defense, Alex held up a hand. "You know what? I need a little space from you right now. I…I need to think about whether this was a big mistake. I should talk to my aunt again."

Disappointment washed over me.

I already saw myself on the next return flight. Without having seen anything of the Scottish Highlands. I hadn't even been inside a castle, for crying out loud!

I was going to remedy that, if it was the last thing I did while I was here.

He wanted me out of the way, anyway.

I held my head up high and said with as much dignity as I could muster, "Fine. I'll go for a walk."

Alex just nodded absentmindedly.

I walked straight out of the garden to the road in front of the house, trying not to cry.

My assumption was that the dirt road would lead to the castle, so I just followed it along its twists and turns.

Once I'd successfully suppressed my tears, anger took over.

I looked the way I looked. There wasn't much I could do about it; nobody had described me as boring before.

And how dare he suggest that this was somehow my fault? He had seen me during the video chat, and he'd known what I looked like!

If he was going to breach our employment contract for that reason, I would insist on getting paid a severance. I wouldn't let Alex push me around like that. In fact, I felt a little duped myself. Maybe I'd sue him.

I was so absorbed in my revenge fantasies that I almost failed to notice the building that appeared between the trees as I walked around a bend.

The castle!

I put Alex out of my mind and walked on in excitement until I got to a large wrought-iron gate. If the gate were open, the sight would have been much the same as in the photograph Alex had sent me.

Now, the black bars were blocking my way.

I rattled the gate, but it was firmly shut.

Hesitating, I slowly walked in a little circle. Now that I'd made it all the way here, I didn't feel like turning around and asking Alex for a key to the gate.

But today would probably be the last chance I had to see the castle up close.

I walked along the wall that surrounded the building. Only the gateposts were really high. The wall itself was low enough for me to peek over if I stood on my tippy toes.

It was still too high to climb over, though. At least without something that could boost me up…

I looked around until I spotted a tree close to the wall.

As I pulled myself up onto a low-hanging branch, a memory from my childhood suddenly resurfaced. My grandparents on my dad's side—we had no contact with my mom's side of the family—owned a farm in Virginia. It was where my brother and I had spent our summers during childhood. There had been countless trees and other opportunities for climbing and similar adventures.

I hadn't climbed a tree in a long while, and nobody would take me for the type who would. But back then, I could best my older brother.

The fun I had with climbing as a child came back to me as I scaled the tree, climbed onto the wall, and then jumped into the long grass on the other side.

If only Alex would have seen me. He wouldn't call me a princess anymore.

Pleased with myself, I stomped through the grass toward the castle. I stopped at the graveled forecourt and looked up at the gray walls of the building.

It was impressive—like a castle in a fairy tale. Although I had to admit that it must have seen better times.

That only added to its rustic, old-world charm in my mind.

It was made of gray rubble stone, which was now covered in moss and ivy. On three corners of the building were bay towers with semi-conical roofs in the same gray slate as the main gable roof.

I sighed. It was a real shame I hadn't been allowed to spend at least one night in the castle. It would have been great to climb a tower and look out one of the windows on the other side—they had to afford a splendid view of Loch Creran, which wasn't far.

Alex had made it sound as if the castle wasn't fit to live in, but maybe I could walk around inside? Provided I could find an open door…

Unsure, I inched closer to the entrance.

Then I backed off, startled, when someone opened the narrow door and came out.

It was a young man in a kilt.

I was standing right there, but he had to be so lost in his thoughts that he didn't appear to notice me.

"Hello?" I said.

The man stopped and stared at me.

Now that I had time to examine him more closely, I noticed his outfit was a little peculiar. It looked like an old-fashioned hunting outfit. Maybe he was dressed up for some sort of ceremony or a historical fair.

I also couldn't help but notice that he was ruggedly handsome. Not as ruggedly handsome as Alex—although his moss-green eyes reminded me a little of my employer. The man had hair the color of sand and a very charming smile, which he now bestowed on me.

Alex had mentioned that the estate belonged not just to him but to his entire family, so I assumed this had to be a relative of his.

"Good morning, lassie," the man said with a strong Scottish accent.

He looked me up and down, settling his gaze on my calves.

"Might I ask where you are off to in this rather…airy dress?" he asked.

The look on his face made it very clear to me that this man didn't think I looked boring at all.

I returned his thousand-watt smile.

"I'm just going for a walk. Please forgive me for intruding, but I must admit that I climbed a tree to get over the wall and see the castle up close. I'm staying in a cottage near here, and…" Unsure, I trailed off, because the man's eyebrows were rising higher and higher.

I couldn't read his expression. Was he dismayed that I'd entered the castle grounds without permission? But he didn't look angry as much as…fascinated.

"You climbed a tree in this dress? I'd love to have seen that."

"Um, well, yeah. Anyway, my name is Bethany. Bethany Prince."

"Euan Campbell. Pleasure to make your acquaintance. Your accent is unusual. Where are you from?"

"Overseas. Boston."

Euan drew his brows together. "Oh. The States. That explains a lot. I heard that you have…different customs over there." His gaze raked over my dress again.

"Yes, I guess there are cultural differences. And you were checking on the castle, I assume?"

"Checking on? I'm the lord of this castle."

"You…live here?" I asked in surprise.

Euan nodded.

My annoyance at Alex rose again. He'd claimed the castle was unoccupied and uninhabitable. He'd clearly been lying. Just because he didn't want me to come here? Or maybe he was ashamed that one of his relatives could actually afford to live here.

I looked up at the castle. I was so curious about what it looked like from the inside. Alex certainly would never show it to me. And I had little to lose. I probably wouldn't be here tomorrow. It couldn't hurt to ask, right?

"I'd love a tour."

"A tour?" Euan seemed confused.

"Um, yes, I'd love to see the inside of the castle. Take a tour of the rooms."

A grin slowly spread across his face. "I see. I wouldn't mind giving you a tour, Miss Prince."

A blush crept up my cheeks. Euan was clearly flirting with me.

But was that such a bad thing? He was an attractive man.

"Great!" I smiled and made a step toward the entrance.

A shadow darkened his eyes. "But unfortunately I can't do that right now. I have an appointment. Maybe…" He hesitated. "Where did you say you were staying? What brought you to Scotland?"

"I'm a muse."

Euan's eyes widened. Then he laughed. "Well, of course you are. Just look at you. Of course you are a muse."

I was about to tell him I worked for a relative of his when Euan continued. "In that case, it would be my pleasure to invite you to the castle this evening. What do you reckon? We'll have dinner, a nice glass of wine, and…I'll give you a tour." He winked at me.

"That would be lovely. What time?"

"Shall we say eight o'clock?"

"Brilliant," I beamed. "I'll be there."

"I'm looking forward to it, Miss Prince."

"Me too. And please, call me Bethany."

"Bethany." He took a step closer and stretched out his hand. For a moment, it looked as if he was about to wrap one of my curls around his finger, but he stopped inches before touching my hair.

There was some sort of electrical current in the air. It was buzzing.

Was that what people meant when they talked about the spark of love at first sight?

I didn't know if I really felt like that—Euan was attractive, charming, and the wealthy castle owner I'd dreamed about, but just because he checked all the boxes, I couldn't say I fell head over heels in love with him.

But maybe this was it. I'd never been in love, so what did I know? There was something going on between us, no doubt about it. The atmosphere was charged, and it felt magical.

"See you later, Bethany."

Euan turned around and disappeared between the trees on the castle grounds.

I stared at the spot for a few seconds before looking around for a good place to climb over the wall again.

I was so exhilarated about this chance encounter that I almost felt like I could jump over the wall!

It didn't matter that Alex had turned out to be a tremendous disappointment.

I had a date!

With a real, distinguished lord of a castle.

My dream was coming true after all.

CHAPTER FIVE

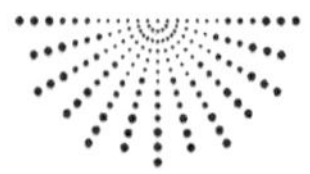

Upon my return to the cottage, I found Alex in the workshop. I said hello but only received a curt nod.

Evidently, he was too absorbed in his work again to talk to me or apologize for his earlier behavior.

I stormed off to my room, angry at myself for even trying with the pompous ass.

Hanging up my dresses in the slim wardrobe calmed me down again. I took my time choosing an outfit for my date with Euan. I wanted to pick something in a similar style and color, just a little fancier.

There was a small mirror above the chest of drawers, but I couldn't really see much of myself in it, so I took it down and placed it at an angle against the wall for my little fashion show.

When I had narrowed down my choice to two outfits, I laid them out on the bed and then went into the bathroom to draw a bath.

The old-fashioned, freestanding bathtub with claw feet was quite suitable for a luxury bath—much more so than taking a shower.

After my beauty routine, I put on yoga pants and a tank top. I'd slip into my date outfit later.

Then I made a pot of tea, found some cookies, and poked my head through the workshop doorway to ask Alex if he wanted to take a break.

I thought it was very mature of me.

He said yes and joined me in the kitchen.

"I met someone on my walk. And I arranged to meet with him tonight. I hope that's not…awkward for you?" I blew on the hot tea and looked at Alex over the rim of my cup.

He frowned. "Did you go all the way to the village? Were you gone that long?"

"No. I was at the castle." I should be glad he didn't seem bothered about me going on a date, but I couldn't help but be a little disappointed.

Alex set his cup down. "What do you mean? Was there someone trespassing on our lands?"

"No." I smiled. "I was the trespasser, I guess. I was right in front of the castle, and he exited it at that moment."

When Alex looked even more puzzled, I explained. "I climbed over the wall, all right? I was curious and wanted to see the building up close."

"Hang on," he interrupted me. "The man came out of the castle? Through the door?"

I tried not to roll my eyes. "Yes, through the door. It's his home, after all. He told me he's the lord of the castle. Listen, I don't know why you thought you had to pretend that it was uninhabitable, but—"

Alex shook his head. "Bethany, nobody lives there. The castle is empty. It's dilapidated. My aunt has the other key, but she lives far away and almost never comes here. She would have definitely told me if she'd sent someone to inspect the building or something like that. This must be a mistake."

"It's no mistake." Anger rose in my chest. Was Alex trying to gaslight me? "He came through the door, told me he lived there, that he's the lord of the castle. He was dressed like it too. And he looked a little like you, so he's a relative."

"Who was he supposed to be?" Alex was getting exasperated too. "Does this mysterious man have a name?"

"Yes! Euan Campbell. Holy cow, you must really have some jealousy issues if you can't even acknowledge the existence of the man who, unlike you, can afford the upkeep of the castle. You really ought to get over this starving artist crap. Living like a vagabond while your cousin or whatever literally lords it over the castle…"

Something in Alex's expression made me trail off.

I noticed he was holding on to the edge of the table, and his knuckles were white.

"Are you quite finished?" There was a dangerous edge to his voice.

I swallowed and nodded.

"Good. You've been taken for a ride, Bethany. Whoever you met at the castle was most definitely not Euan Campbell. He's an ancestor of mine and has been dead for almost a hundred years. There are rumors that his ghost is forever destined to haunt the castle. The castle is famous for its spookiness, thanks to Euan, in fact. But if you talked to him and he asked you out on a date, it can't have been Sir Euan's ghost." Alex sounded cynical.

"I suspect someone familiar with the ghost stories was having a little fun with you. I can well imagine how you batted your lashes at him because you thought he was a rich lord of the castle. He probably thought, what the heck, let's see how gullible this naive American girl is." He relaxed and started laughing. "Incredibly gullible, it turns out. The more I think about it, the more I've gotta hand it to him. It is one hell of a prank."

Alex could barely get his words out, he was laughing so hard. He was holding his sides. "Sir Euan Campbell asking you out on a date. Hahahaha."

I, too, could hardly speak. But it wasn't because I thought any of this was funny. No, I certainly wasn't laughing. I was livid.

"I know what I saw and what I heard," I got out between clenched teeth. "I'm not completely clueless."

Alex was laughing louder, and he was now slapping the tabletop for good measure.

I raised my voice. "He invited me to dinner. At the castle. If it really were empty, his little prank wouldn't work out that well, would it? I would immediately catch on to the fact that he's not Euan Campbell. So what would the alleged prankster gain from this, huh?"

"You…want to…dine with him in the castle?" Alex wheezed, tears streaming down his face. "You actually plan on going up there tonight, all dressed up, aren't you? Wait, wait." He got up and grabbed a large old-fashioned key from the keyboard on the wall. "You'd better take that, or you won't get in. It's the only way to convince you, it seems. You'll see that the castle is not in a state for anyone to live there. You'll see that this man…"

I snatched the key from his hand. I fully expected Euan to be there to let me in, but it couldn't hurt to have the key. I would have a look inside the castle this evening, come hell or high water.

I didn't know if I could believe a word that came out of my employer's mouth anymore. But I knew I could trust my own senses. The person who had asked me out on a date had access to the castle and looked like a relative of Alex's. There was still the small possibility that this relative had been leading me on, wanting me to believe he was the castle owner.

Either way, I'd find out. And I wouldn't let myself be made a laughingstock.

"Be careful, though." Alex's tone had changed. "Maybe this is more than a harmless prank. What kind of man wants to lure a young woman to a secluded, abandoned building like that? Come to think of it, maybe you shouldn't—"

I jumped up. "Oh no, you don't. Don't you dare try to convince me not to go on the date so you can continue to gaslight me. Pretending to be a chivalrous protector, no less. That mask doesn't suit you, Alex. Believe it or not, I'm an adult—not a naive girl—and I can make up my own mind. I don't know what your endgame is here—to manipulate me, to intimidate me, whatever. But you've chosen the wrong woman for your games, Alex."

Dismay spread across his face. In fact, he looked pretty shocked.

But I didn't know how good an actor Alexander Campbell was, and right now, I didn't even care.

I saw there was another key on the board with the label "Gate" on it, and I took that too.

"I'm going on this date tonight, and don't you dare try to stop me." With these words, I grabbed my mug of tea and sashayed out of the kitchen, trying to look more confident than I felt.

CHAPTER SIX

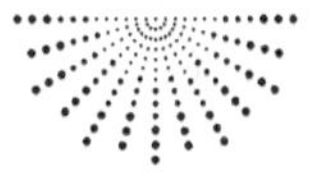

I sat down on the bed in my room. There wasn't really any other option, since the room was too small for an extra chair.

Trying to calm myself down, I finished my tea.

I was playing around on my phone when it rang. It was my mother.

I was tempted to decline the call. My mother had the uncanny ability to pick up how I was feeling over the phone, no matter how hard I tried to sound as if everything was fine. I wasn't in the mood for an "I told you so."

But I'd only sent a quick text yesterday, to let my parents know I'd arrived safely. They'd want a more detailed report, and I figured I'd rather deal with that sooner than later.

"Hi, Mom!" I put on a cheerful voice to give a brief account of the trip and my arrival.

To my surprise, my mother seemed far less perceptive than usual. I soon found out it was because she had something on her mind she was dying to tell me.

"Our ancestors are from close to where you're staying. Imagine that!"

"Huh? Our ancestors?"

"I had a chat with Beatrice yesterday. You know, the cousin who got in touch a while ago?"

Mom had grown up in a foster family, and she hadn't had contact with her biological family until recently. Her mother—my grandmother—had been a teenage runaway before becoming pregnant with my mother. She'd been mentally ill, and it got worse after Mom's birth, so she'd ended up in a hospital.

Mom entered the system but was soon placed with a very nice foster family. She stayed with them until she finished school, and although she kept in contact with Grandma, she kind of considered her foster parents her actual family.

Mom never found out who her father was, and her mother had only ever briefly mentioned a brother, no other family members.

But recently, Gran's brother's daughter had found Mom through a heritage site. They visited each other and kept in touch via phone and email.

"When I told Bea you were in Scotland, she explained our grandmother emigrated from Scotland as a young woman."

Mom's voice trembled a little, as usual, when she talked about her biological family. She was a tough woman, but her family's past was a sore subject with her.

"All right, so my great-grandmother was Scottish?" I was very pleased to hear that. I felt like running into the workshop and doing a little dance, singing "I'm not an American princess, but a Scot, like you."

"Yes. As you know, Bea is doing genealogical research, and she found out that your great-grandmother came from a village named Tarbet in the Scottish Highlands! I looked it up on the map, and it's very close to where you are."

I rolled my eyes. "Mom, everything in Scotland is really close."

"No, I'm serious. Have a look on the map."

"All right, I will. Tarbet, did you say?"

"Yes. Maybe you could take a little trip and visit the place our ancestors are from."

I still wasn't sure how much longer I would be employed, and I was determined to make the most of what might be my one and only opportunity to visit Scotland. "You know what? I think I'll do that."

"Oh, great. You could take pictures and send them to me." Mom sounded so excited. Her reservations about me taking this job and going all the way to Scotland by myself seemed to have gone out the window.

"Sure, I can do that. Do you have any more information? Our great-grandmother's maiden name, for example? Maybe we still have relatives in Tarbet."

"Oh, good thinking! I'll ask Bea right away. She'd know."

"Great. Mom, I have to go. I have to get ready for a date."

"A date? Who did you meet in a such a short space of time to go on a date with? It's not your employer, is it?" Her disapproval was obvious in her voice.

I laughed. "No, certainly not. It's someone else I met today."

"Okay, well, have fun. And be careful."

"Yes, Mom. Goodbye."

I hung up, wishing she hadn't added the last bit. She was just being a protective mother, but it reminded me of Alex's warning.

And both of them might be right to be concerned.

Going to meet someone I didn't know in a secluded place…

Angrily, I brushed away the paranoid thoughts.

Euan was clearly a relative of Alex's, so my employer knew him, no matter how much he pretended otherwise. Whatever Alex's endgame was in gaslighting me, if he was really concerned for my safety, he should be straight with me.

I grabbed the less revealing of the two outfits I had chosen earlier. The top was fifties style, a bit like the dress I'd worn earlier, with blue and white dots, a sweetheart neckline, and short, puffy sleeves. It looked best with skinny jeans, and luckily, I'd brought a pair that made my legs look great. A bonus was that this outfit could be paired with flat shoes, which would make walking to the castle much easier.

I tied my hair in a ponytail with a red scarf, put on large hoop earrings, and opted for red lipstick to give me confidence.

One last look in the mirror, and I was out the door.

I felt ready for my date with a lord of a castle, but I couldn't shake off a bad feeling.

Inwardly, I cursed Alex for getting into my head like that.

I didn't even say goodbye to him.

All the way to the castle, the premonition that something bad would happen just wouldn't dissipate.

CHAPTER SEVEN

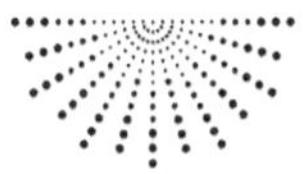

Despite the feeling of dread that was growing by the minute, I didn't turn around.

I wasn't merely spooked by what Alex and my mom had said.

I also realized that, even though it was still light out on this June evening, later, on my way back, it would be pitch black. I hadn't brought a flashlight. At least I had my phone, even though I wasn't sure how well it was charged.

To top things off, when I got to the bend in the road where the castle became visible, there was no light shining through any of the windows. It looked completely deserted. Nervously, I told myself that it was a summer evening, and lights inside weren't needed. This was just Alex messing with my head, wasn't it?

I should have listened to my intuition, which clearly told me something was off, but I was too proud to go back and admit to my employer that he had been right. It really irked me that Alex took me for a naive girl who would fall for such high jinks—or would be taken in by something worse than a harmless prank—and I wanted to prove him wrong.

So I held on to the hope in my heart that charming lord of the castle Euan would prove to be who he'd claimed to be.

With trembling fingers, I unlocked the iron gate, and it opened with an ominous creak.

I hesitated, then pushed the gate closed behind me and made my way to the entrance door. The walls of the castle loomed above me as I grabbed the old-fashioned knob and turned it. It wouldn't budge, though. I pressed against the door, but it was firmly shut.

My heart was pounding, even though my brain tried to convince it that this didn't have to mean anything. So Euan had locked the door. That was only sensible.

After looking in vain for something like a doorbell, I knocked. Tentatively at first, then more forcefully.

"Euan?" My voice sounded squeaky, and I cleared my throat. "Euan? Hello? It's me, Bethany."

The only answer was an eerie silence. Even the birds had stopped singing. Dark clouds had moved across the sky, erasing the glow of the evening sun, so it was suddenly quite gloomy.

I shivered.

"Euan?"

I thought I heard a faint bark. Pressing my ear against the door, I strained to listen. Was there a dog inside the castle? Euan's dog?

But the barking stopped.

Turning around in a circle, I chewed my lip.

I still wasn't ready to give up and go home. What I couldn't understand was why "Euan" had done this to me. Standing me up like this was a mean joke, but what did he have to gain from it?

He wouldn't even get to see my reaction.

Or was he hiding somewhere close, watching me?

My gaze darted around in panic. Goosebumps were covering my arms, and I hugged myself.

Then I pulled myself together. It was bad enough that I would have to go crawling back to Alex, admitting to him he had been right.

I wouldn't give this Euan character the satisfaction.

Yes, he had been the sort of dashing man I saw myself with, and I had been excited about the date. But more so, I had wanted a tour of the castle.

Determined, I dug the key to the front door out of my red clutch. Fake Euan wouldn't keep me from seeing the inside of this building.

I had to admit that deep inside my heart there was a last vestige of hope that Euan was somewhere in the castle where he hadn't heard my knocks, maybe putting the finishing touches to the romantic dinner he'd set up in one of the ostentatious castle rooms.

Taking a deep breath, I put the key in the lock and turned it. My heart was beating like crazy in my chest when I pushed the door open.

There was nothing but darkness inside.

I fumbled for my phone and turned on the flashlight app.

There wasn't much to see.

I was in a small entrance hall with a stone floor, stone walls, and hardly any furniture.

There was a door opposite the entrance, and I opened it.

I stepped into another, bigger hall. This one had furniture, but it was covered with sheets.

I lifted the corner of one, noticing how dusty it was. Underneath, I discovered a Chesterfield sofa in dire need of repair.

I dropped the sheet and stepped toward the enormous stone fireplace, which seemed impressive from afar. But when I got close, I noticed how crumbly the stone was. Oak panels covered the bottom half of the walls to the left and right of the fireplace—possibly wainscoting the entire room. They were old and full of wormholes.

Steps led to another raised level of the hall, but they seemed so rotten that I didn't dare go up there. From what I could see, there was just more covered furniture. The sheet had slipped from a three-legged chair, and I thought I could make out more chairs and tables underneath the sheets. Maybe this was a dining area.

There were thick curtains in front of the windows, and I considered letting in the evening light, but I was afraid to touch them in case the moth-eaten fabric would come down on me.

It wasn't even necessary to illuminate this room—and the truth—even more.

Nobody was living in this castle. It had been left to fall apart a long time ago.

Alex had been right.

It should have been enough to make me leave and return to the cottage.

But something about this old castle just wouldn't let me leave. Maybe it was the centuries of history that clung to the walls like the layers of dust.

I'd felt something similar in historic buildings at home—only they were never this old. And I definitely knew the feeling on a smaller scale from antiques. I'd often noticed something like an electric charge when I touched old furniture or objects, a crackle that I'd always interpreted as a sign that old artifacts and I belonged together.

What I experienced in this castle was so much more than a humming or a crackle. It was a roar.

No matter what the explanation, my feet carried me up the grand staircase at the other end of the room, as if drawn there by a magnet.

I even imagined a voice beckoning me—a soft, whispering voice that I shouldn't really be able to hear over the background holler.

There were lots of broken steps beyond the first floor, which seemed very unsafe to climb, so I turned into a small foyer. It was dark, and I lifted my phone with the flashlight app.

Startled, I took a step back. I thought a fox was going to pounce on me, and it felt as if my heart was about to jump out of my chest.

But on second look, I realized the fox wasn't alive. It was a taxidermied animal mounted on the wall.

It was in good company.

As I let the narrow light beam travel across the room, I saw a whole range of birds and small woodland creatures. Some seemed half-finished or torn apart, with missing limbs and straw and sawdust spilling out.

The sight made my stomach turn, and I quickly crossed the foyer, following the now louder voice, beckoning me to a spindly iron staircase.

The wrought-iron banister wobbled dangerously as I carefully climbed one narrow step after the other.

I paused in front of a dark door.

Whatever had been calling me was in this room.

It was dark and forbidden, and part of me wanted to run away. But another part just had to open the door, no matter what might happen. There was something delicious about following my desire…my urges…that had no rhyme or reason.

Ordinarily, I wasn't a thrill seeker. As a child, I'd never been a goody-two-shoes either. My grandma, a proper Southern lady, used to describe me as a little wild sometimes. But I think anyone would say that I was a good girl.

I'd never tried drugs, but I imagined that this was what it felt like to be addicted to such a substance. You really,

really wanted it. You knew it would lead to ruin, but you were powerless in the face of your desire.

I must have had an inkling about what was behind the door. I remembered at the time, my trembling fingers on the doorknob, I fantasized Euan had called me there. In my mind's eye, I had seen a four-poster bed in gleaming mahogany, covered in a canopy made from thick red-and-gold jacquard. The duvet matched the ostentatious fabric and patterns.

I'd seen myself opening the curtains in front of the tower window and looking out at the gray waters of Loch Creran, framed by the mountains beyond.

I'd felt Euan approach me from behind, wrap his arms around me. I'd even felt his warm breath before he placed a tender kiss on a sensitive spot on my neck.

It was such a strong and vivid vision, even though I couldn't have known what was in the room.

The only thing I knew for certain was that Euan didn't exist.

Alex hadn't lied. He hadn't tried to gaslight me.

He'd spoken the truth: Euan Campbell was long dead.

Yet, I'd met him. I'd spoken to him.

That could only mean one thing…

But it was insane. It simply couldn't be.

I felt a little faint. Oh god, no!

A loud noise snapped me out of my frantic state, and I let go of the doorknob, as if the metal had suddenly turned red hot and singed my hand.

Whirling around, I grabbed hold of the banister, but the staircase started shaking, and I felt even more disoriented.

I heard the clatter again from somewhere below.

Carefully and slowly, I climbed down the spiral staircase.

Fear crept up inside of me, pushing aside all the

conflicting emotions that had been center stage only a moment ago.

There was someone else in the castle.

Alex's warning rang in my ears.

What if the man I'd met earlier had been a real person, after all? Someone who had impersonated Euan Campbell.

That was a much more likely scenario than what I'd just thought of.

What if this man had lured me here so he could do unspeakable things to me?

I would have liked to avoid turning on my flashlight app, but the floorboards in the creepy foyer were a real stumbling hazard. I didn't want to have my foot get stuck in a rotten board and hurt myself, twisting an ankle or worse.

So I pointed the beam at the floor and slowly crept forward.

I tried to listen for any telltale noises, but there was that roar again, although this time, it might have been caused by the blood rushing in my ears.

When the light fell on a pair of shoes, I let out a loud scream.

I was so shocked, I dropped my phone.

In sheer panic, I tried to dart past the man with the shoes, but he grabbed me with strong arms.

Continuing to shriek, I fought him off with all my strength, until he whispered in my ear, "Shhh. Stop fighting."

CHAPTER EIGHT

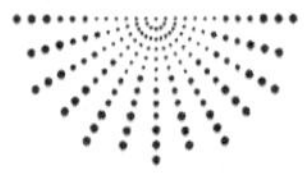

"Everything's all right."

I stopped fighting and went limp when I recognized Alex's voice. It was he who was holding me.

He'd come to save me from whatever or whoever was threatening me inside the walls of this castle.

I let Alex stroke my hair while my panicked breath turned into quiet sobs.

"I'm sorry I scared you. I was so worried. I didn't want to interfere. It's not my place, I get that. You are a grown woman. But I worked myself up into a frenzy, and I just had to come to make sure you're all right. What kind of guy would lure a pretty lass like yourself to an abandoned building at night? I didn't want anything to happen to you."

"It's okay," I said, wiping my tears away. "I'm glad you came. Let's get out of here."

"Of course. Come on, let me help you." Alex took my arm to lead me to the stairs. He switched on the flashlight app on his phone. "Oh, it really is dark in here."

This reminded me of my own phone.

"My cell. I dropped it." I turned around but froze at the thought of going back into the creepy room with the taxidermied animals.

"Wait here. I'll get it." Alex left me standing where I was and went back to find my phone.

I wrapped my arms around my middle, feeling very lonely all of a sudden.

Luckily, it didn't take long before he shouted, "I've got it," and came back.

Alex put his arm around my waist, and I leaned on him as we left the gloomy castle.

I breathed in the fresh evening air and instantly felt much better.

When Alex closed the gate behind us, I said, "Thank you. I mean it. Thank you for coming here and protecting me. You were right. It really was naive of me to believe that man who'd claimed to be Euan Campbell. But I really wanted to see the inside of a Scottish castle. And to be honest, I didn't want to believe that someone might play such a cruel joke on me."

Alex frowned. "I don't really understand it either, especially since he wasn't here, was he?"

I shook my head.

"Well, some people just have a sick sense of humor, I suppose. Come on, let's go home."

I rubbed my arms, still covered in goosebumps. "Yes, please."

"You're cold. Hang on." Alex took off his hoodie and gave it to me.

The washed-out hoodie in a nondescript color ordinarily wouldn't have been my style, but now I took it gladly.

The soft cotton felt wonderful against my skin. Slipping

on the hoodie was almost like having Alex's arm around my waist. It made me feel safe.

"Did you take the key?" Alex pointed at the gate.

I felt my cheeks go warm. "Oh. Um. Yes. Sorry."

"That's okay. But where did you put it? The key to the castle entrance was still stuck in the lock…" He dug it out of his jeans pocket and showed it to me. "But the gate key…?"

I touched my own pockets, but then I remembered. "The clutch! I put it in the clutch."

Alex looked confused.

"It's a handbag. I must have lost it somewhere inside. Probably on the spiral staircase." The thought sent an icy shiver down my spine. "I don't want to go back." The panic in my voice was clearly audible. "Please, Alex, I can't go back in there."

"It's all right, we don't have to. We'll leave the gate unlocked for now, and I'll go back and search for it tomorrow."

I nodded with relief.

Then we hurried back to the cottage to get home before dusk fully set in.

Inside, Alex wished me a good night.

"Alex…" I hesitated but then said what was on my mind. "I'm too scared to be alone. Would you mind staying up with me for a little while?"

Alex looked at me for a moment. "Sure. No problem. Why don't I make us a pot of tea and light the lantern in the garden? It's a nice evening to sit outside."

"I'll take care of the tea," I said, happy to occupy myself with a task, and marched into the kitchen.

When I came outside with a tray full of tea and shortbread, I followed a path illuminated by old-fashioned lanterns. It led around the cottage to the other side of the workshop. I hadn't explored this area yet and was delighted to see a small, tiled terrace surrounded by a slightly less unkempt garden than on the other side. Pink roses ranged up the stone walls of the cottage on this side, and it took me a moment to orient myself. The small window on the right had to be my bedroom window. Alex's bedroom was next to it, so the French windows that opened up onto the terrace led to his room.

There was a small round table with an inset ceramic mosaic scene flanked by two rattan armchairs, and there were lanterns on all four corners of the terrace.

It looked enchanting.

I put the tray down on the garden table, poured us tea, and then sat down in one of the chairs.

Alex, who had just gotten himself another sweater from his room, plunked himself down on the other one.

We sat in comfortable silence, drinking our tea and eating chocolate shortbread.

Then Alex put his cup down and cleared his throat. "Sorry again for giving you such a fright in the castle. I came to make sure you were all right, and then I… completely traumatized you."

"No you didn't. I mean, yes, you scared me, but I was already freaked out, so your sudden appearance was just what sent me over the edge."

"What freaked you out? The sudden realization that you wouldn't meet Prince Charming in the castle after all?"

"Stop!" I shot him a dirty look over the rim of my teacup. "That's not it. Okay, I admit I had romantic notions when I came here. But it wasn't just about some shallow fairy-tale ideas, okay? I longed for the chance to see the inside of a Scottish castle. I studied art history, and I specialize in antiques. I'm really interested in all of that."

"Oh. Of course," Alex said ruefully. "You should have told me. I would have shown you around."

I lifted an eyebrow. "Really?"

"Okay, okay, I admit I pigeonholed you, based on your suitcase, your clothes, your entire demeanor when you arrived here…"

"I guess I can't fault you for that," I grumbled. "My outfit choice was a tad inappropriate." I shrugged. "I just like to dress nicely. I like beautiful things, and I have a keen eye for aesthetics. That's not a crime."

"It's not," Alex admitted. "As an artist, I should understand that better, I guess. But I'm interested in true beauty that's more than…dress-up deep, do you understand?"

I could have easily felt insulted by that—and if he'd said it at another moment, I might have been—but now I just had to laugh.

"Why'd you pick a shallow American who doesn't understand true beauty like a real artist, then?" I said mockingly.

Alex put his hands over his face. "Oh my god. I sound really pretentious, don't I?"

"Yes!"

He had to laugh now too.

"You know what? I think it would do you good not to take yourself too seriously, and maybe not take your art so seriously either. When was the last time you approached your work with a sense of play? Fun, even?"

Alex stared at me. "Wow."

I blushed, hiding my face behind the cup as I drank the last of the tea. "I'm sorry if that was too forward…"

"No," Alex said. "I probably needed to hear it." He rubbed his chin. "Now that we've cleared the air, why don't you tell me about what scared you so much at the castle?"

I took a deep breath and put the cup down on the tray.

Staring at the lantern at the far right of the veranda instead of looking at Alex, I began to explain. "I had a strange feeling as soon as I entered the castle. It felt as if something was drawing me toward it. It was like a pull toward this room on top of the smaller tower, the one the spiral staircase at the end of the room with the animals leads to. And in front of that door, I had…I guess you'd call it an episode. Like a hallucination."

"This castle has a way of sparking people's imagination," Alex interrupted. "I already told you, it's haunted. People have reported seeing and feeling all sorts of things in there. From a barking dog to an old woman serving them imaginary tea. And the ghost of Euan Campbell, obviously. So don't worry too much about it."

"No. It's not that I'm scared of silly ghost stories or anything like that." I shifted my position in the rattan chair and looked right into Alex's eyes. "Mental illness runs in my family. Nobody likes to talk about it…and, well, my mother hardly has any contact with my grandmother, but…yeah, that's the reason my mother was placed into foster care as a child. Grandma was committed to an institution… I think she went in and out of the hospital a bunch of times. I don't know what her diagnosis is, exactly, but Mom did say Grandma saw things that weren't there."

I closed my eyes, thinking of what I had fantasized about in front of that door. In other circumstances, I might have called it a daydream, yet I knew it had been so much more than that.

"Anyway," I tried to come back to the present, "since Mom got in touch with a cousin, we've learned more about that side of our family. And it turns out that other female relatives had similar problems, so yeah… Like I said, that kind of thing seems to run in the family. I never had any… issues before. So I never worried about being afflicted. Until now."

"Hmm. It's true that one can be genetically predisposed to have a mental illness. But I know that, statistically speaking, the first signs of such a psychotic break or symptoms of paranoid schizophrenia usually show up much earlier in life. It's unlikely that you really would have had your first episode at your age, in a dark, spooky castle in Scotland. It's possible. But it's more likely it had to do with an overwrought imagination and being in said dark, spooky castle."

"Yes, you're probably right." I chewed my lips. What he said sounded reasonable. But I had no way of explaining the strange sensation of...desire I'd felt. The promise of something intoxicating.

"I think we should both go back together. We'll find your handbag, and then we'll draw back the curtains to let some light into the castle. That should dispel any 'ghosts'." He made air quotes. "I think it would be a good idea if you went into that room, see for yourself that it was just nerves and a propensity to fantasize and romanticize."

The thought of doing that turned my heart into an ice block. My throat closed, and I couldn't say anything.

I just nodded. Facing my fears would probably be the best idea. And I'd have Alex by my side.

I could see that underneath his rough exterior there was a kindhearted man. Thinking about that made my heart melt again.

Before coming here, I'd built up Alex as a knight in shining armor. I'd been disappointed to have my expectations squashed.

But it had served me right.

And, in fact, the real Alex who was emerging was a lot better than anything I could have romanticized about.

He was more of a knight in a worn hoodie, but so what? It had never really been about wealth for me. True, I had a thing for well-dressed men, but for Alex, I could be flexible.

I pulled the sweatshirt up to my nose and breathed in

Alex's scent that clung to the fabric. It was fresh, but also a little mineral, like the stones he worked with.

Butterflies fluttered in my stomach, and I turned to smile at Alex.

"I appreciate you wanting to help me. I think we both had…preconceptions of each other. It's no surprise that the whole muse thing didn't work. But I feel things are changing now that we've gotten to know each other a little better. Let's just start fresh tomorrow. What do you say? Clean slate?"

"Umm. To be honest, I've already made a decision about our working relationship. I informed my aunt, and we discussed ending your employment."

"What?"

Suddenly, I was freezing again. Still, I pulled off the hoodie.

"Yes, but my aunt seems to think we shouldn't give up that easily. She insists that we both speak to her first. She doesn't like to travel, so we'd have to go to her. I told her we'd visit her tomorrow."

"I don't know what your aunt could say to you, considering you've already made your decision," I said. "But sure. I welcome the chance to see a little more of Scotland before I have to go home again."

I stood up and dumped the sweatshirt in Alex's lap. "I'm tired, so I'd better go to bed. Thanks for staying up and listening to me. I hope it wasn't too much of a chore."

"Bethany, I'm sorry—"

"No, it's okay." I forced a smile. "It's been a long day. I just want to go to bed now." Sighing, I added, "Where are we going tomorrow, exactly? I want to look it up in my travel guide."

"Oh, I don't know if it's in there. It's not exactly a tourist hot spot. But it's a lovely, picturesque little place," he added when he saw the disappointment on my face. After so much of it in the last few minutes, I just couldn't hide it any longer.

"And it's on the shore of Loch Lomond, so you'll see the famous loch with the boundary fault separating the Highlands from the Lowlands. My aunt lives in Tarbet."

CHAPTER NINE

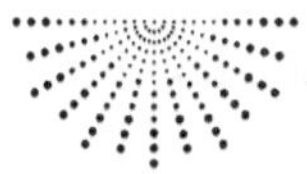

The next day, on the train to Tarbet, I still couldn't believe that Alex's aunt lived in the same village my ancestors supposedly came from.

Could this really be a coincidence?

I hadn't said anything to Alex because, after everything that had happened since my arrival, I didn't know what to believe anymore.

"You seem distracted," Alex said. "Is everything all right?"

"Hmm? Oh. Yes. I'm just…enjoying the scenery." I looked out the window again and this time really tried to focus on the landscape.

I'd been upset about not seeing anything of the Highlands before being sent back home, and now I wasn't even paying attention. And we were traveling on the historic West Highland Railway, which connected Oban with Tarbet.

So for the rest of the journey I did my best to stay present and enjoy the view.

The Tarbet train station was a little outside the village

—in fact, it was between Tarbet and Arrochar, the next village on the shore of Loch Long. I learned that there was a two-mile isthmus of land linking the West Coast and Loch Lomond.

To my disappointment, we didn't walk to the village of Tarbet or even to the shore of Loch Lomond. Instead, we stopped at a restaurant close to the station.

It was an old, renovated church that was aptly named The Kirk. I took a lot of photos of the outside of the stunning building and continued snapping away on my phone as we walked inside. The old church organ was still in the foyer, and the stained glass windows were just stunning.

I knew I behaved just like the New-World tourist I was, but I didn't know whether I'd have many more opportunities for sightseeing.

There was a quaint bar in the foyer and even a little bookshop stall selling Scottish cookbooks. Before I had a chance to browse, Alex led me up a couple of steps to the former nave of the church, which was now the restaurant's dining area.

Alex's aunt, who was supposed to meet us there, hadn't arrived yet. I was getting nervous, but I distracted myself with the menu. I was excited about trying traditional Scottish cuisine, and I didn't know what to choose.

We ordered drinks and were served complimentary homemade bread and delicious trout mousse while we waited.

I knew when Alex's aunt finally arrived, even though I was sitting with my back to the entrance.

Everyone's attention seemed to shift to the person who entered. I saw raised eyebrows and heard people whisper.

A warm smile spread across Alex's face, and he stood up. "Aunt Mary!"

I turned around—and promptly spat out a sip of water I'd just taken.

"Everything all right?" Alex asked, patting my back.

"Yes," I pretended to cough. I grabbed the napkin and dabbed my face carefully so as to not smear my make-up.

The napkin also served as a shield to hide my face so that I could get control over my facial expression.

I now understood the lunch crowd's peculiar reaction.

Alex's aunt could have easily been mistaken for a homeless person.

I'd imagined a wealthy patron of the arts in stylish designer clothes. Instead, she was dressed in a baggy, long-sleeved dress made of a thick cloth of an indeterminable dark color. Aside from the fact that it seemed completely inappropriate for a nice summer day, it also looked as if she'd been sleeping and eating in it for decades.

To top it off, Alex's aunt had a mass of tangled black hair that she'd unsuccessfully attempted to tame with a red and yellow flower-patterned scarf. You could say the red matched her lipstick and the yellow her teeth.

She had make-up on, but it looked a little like the work of a mortician desperately trying to make a dead body appear alive.

Which wasn't so farfetched, because Alex's aunt seemed old enough to be a corpse. In fact, she did look a bit like she was dressed up for a Scottish version of the Day of the Dead festival.

"Bethany Prince," I introduced myself after I'd taken far too much time to recover. "Nice to meet you."

"Mary MacDonald. The pleasure is all mine."

Mrs. MacDonald's voice didn't match her appearance at all. It sounded young and melodic, with a soft Scottish accent.

Alex's aunt sat down, and the server came over to take our food order. I asked Mrs. MacDonald what was good and then just ordered what she recommended.

I didn't regret it.

The starter—scallops—was delicious. We'd stuck to polite chitchat until it arrived, but as soon as Mrs. MacDonald had polished off her plate, she got down to business.

She took a folder out of an old canvas bag she'd brought along.

"What has Alex told you about his work so far, Bethany?"

I looked at Alex with uncertainty. "Umm, not much, actually. I saw his workshop when I arrived, but... I guess all I know is what I learned from his website." I didn't mention that it wasn't a lot, since his website was very minimal.

Mrs. MacDonald looked at Alex with disapproval in her eyes. "You haven't even taken the time to explain your process to her?"

Alex shifted uneasily in his chair. "I didn't see the benefit in it. It's not like she could give me any professional advice. She's just an art history graduate, not a sculptor."

I knew he was being defensive, so I tried not to let his remark hurt me.

Mrs. MacDonald closed the folder again. "Alex. You haven't even given her a chance, have you?"

Her tone was like that of a strict, old-fashioned schoolteacher, and I myself sat ramrod straight, as if I'd been the one who'd been reprimanded.

Alex dropped his head and mumbled something that sounded like "sorry."

Mrs. MacDonald sighed. "All right." She opened the folder again and pulled a few photocopies out.

"Here are pictures of Alex's early work. As you can see, Bethany, he worked slowly but steadily toward the sculptures that won him awards: the Modern Scottish Venus series. This is Scottish limestone, his favorite material."

She showed me pictures I'd already seen on the website. I didn't know that much about sculptures, but Alex's work reminded me of the famous American artist Paige Bradley. Her bronze sculptures were more delicate and graceful than the Scottish sculptor's carved stonework, but I remembered a picture of Bradley's Expansion sculpture of a woman in a lotus position in front of the Manhattan skyline.

Her expanding consciousness manifested itself in cracks in her torso, and through the cracks, an internal lighting system shone like the light of the sun, symbolizing inner enlightenment.

Alex had achieved a similar effect with the natural impurities of the limestone. Lines ran across the Venus torso like fine cracks, lending her a fragility that formed a stark contrast to the robust material of the stone.

Alex's aunt pulled a few more photocopies out of her folder. "These are photos of Alexander's more recent work. He sold some sculptures to private clients. Then he found out that they put them in their gardens, and he felt a little…I guess you could say misunderstood. He has since refused to sell his work."

Alex shrank more and more in his seat.

"What do you think, Bethany?"

I glanced in Alex's direction again. He clearly already felt humiliated, and I didn't want to hurt him even more.

I bent over to study the photocopies, even though I'd already formed an opinion.

The sculptures were essentially copies of his famous Venus, but they lacked a certain something. They seemed a little…coarse.

"I think the craftsmanship is excellent," I began slowly. "Alex clearly knows what he's doing. But, umm, there's no progress. In fact, I think these represent a regression, more than anything. Art has to change constantly, as life inevitably changes. These more recent sculptures just don't seem as alive to me."

When I saw Alex's face, I quickly tried to backpedal. "That's just my opinion, though, and I'm not an expert. Maybe I'm talking nonsense. Sorry!"

"No, I think you're spot-on," Mrs. MacDonald said. "Alex works incredibly hard. But he buries himself in his work. And since he hasn't been able to build on his success, he's become more and more of a hermit. Where is the life supposed to come from that must inform your art if you're hardly living, Alex?"

"I think you're exaggerating, Aunt Mary." Alex's nostrils quivered. "Besides, my work *is* my life."

"Yes." Mrs. MacDonald patted Alex's arm. "I know that. That's why I want to help you. You have to admit you're stuck, though."

Alex gave an exasperated sigh. "Okay, yes. But I still don't know how a muse is supposed to help with that. I mean, inspiration can't be forced. And neither can a relationship between artist and muse. Don't artists usually find their muse by felicitous accident? Bethany and I, we're... like fire and water. We have nothing in common. This just isn't working."

Now I couldn't help but look as hurt as I felt.

Like his aunt had said, Alex hadn't really given me a fair chance.

Besides, we weren't that different. It's not like we had nothing in common. And last night, we had vibed. Or had I only imagined that too?

"I think it's a good thing that you're like fire and water," Mrs. MacDonald now said. "I've chosen Bethany as your muse partly because she's vivacious, full of life. She's exactly what you need. Someone who pushes you out of your comfort zone. So you rub each other the wrong way? Great! You should rub against each other."

I blushed as this conjured up an image in my mind that differed greatly from what Mrs. MacDonald had meant.

At least her tone hadn't sounded suggestive at all, but now I saw a twinkle in her eyes, and I wasn't so sure.

Before I could think about it further, the server interrupted with the main course.

It gave us the opportunity to calm down and gather our thoughts.

Mrs. MacDonald put the photocopies away, and we turned the topic of conversation back to the food with regional ingredients.

Alex finally steered us back to the reason we were meeting.

"I understand what you're saying, Auntie. And you're right that I didn't give this a fair chance." He looked at me, and I got butterflies in my stomach. "I didn't give *you* a fair chance, Bethany. I'm sorry. You are very different from me, and I wouldn't have chosen you as a muse, but it's not like I don't like you or would hate to spend time with you."

"Well, thank you very much," I said drily, not sure if I should feel flattered or insulted.

"But how is this supposed to work in a practical sense, Aunt Mary? How can Bethany help me? I already tried to draw her, but…"

"No, no, don't start with art. Start by forgetting about art. Just do things with Bethany. Fun things. Things you normally wouldn't do. Go to a bar, or dancing, or whatever you young folks do this day and age."

"In Oban?" Alex asked skeptically. "It's not exactly famous for its nightlife."

"It doesn't matter," Mrs. MacDonald waved off his reservations. "Just go out together. Experience something."

Alex rubbed his face. "All right. I guess. It won't hurt to try." He shook his head. "It doesn't feel right to abandon my work when things aren't going so great. It feels an awful lot like procrastination. But I admit hard work hasn't really gotten me very far."

"Good," Mrs. MacDonald said with a satisfied smile. "Then that's settled. Bethany is going to stay, and the two of you are going to go out and have a great time."

I felt a stone the size of one of Alex's Venus sculptures roll off my heart. I was a bit surprised at myself. Even though I'd been a little pissed off about having to leave Scotland before really seeing much of it, I hadn't been that concerned about ending my working relationship with a pompous artist who wasn't my Prince Charming after all.

Feeling so relieved about staying on as Alex's muse opened my eyes to how I really felt. But I wasn't ready to think about that right now.

I had other things to discuss with Mrs. MacDonald.

Luckily, Alex gave me the opportunity to do just that when he got up.

"Please don't take this the wrong way, but I need some fresh air. I'd like to take a walk on my own and get my thoughts in order. You dished out some bitter truths for me to swallow, Auntie."

"I know," Mrs. MacDonald said softly and patted Alex's hand. "Of course you're excused. Go for your walk. Bethany and I are going to have dessert, won't we, lass?"

I just nodded.

"See you later," Alex said and left, sending the server over on his way out.

She recommended raspberry cranachan, a traditional Scottish dessert made with cream, cream cheese, crumbled oatmeal cookies, and raspberry compote. The frozen version, which was served in The Kirk, came with little pieces of meringue.

Once we'd placed our order, I turned to Mrs. MacDonald.

Even though I was nervous as hell, I looked her right in the eyes and said, "Now that we're alone, you can tell me the real reason I'm here. Why you chose me for the job and invited me to Scotland."

CHAPTER TEN

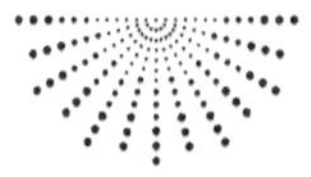

Mrs. MacDonald looked at me with her shrewd, dark eyes. "Why do *you* think you're here?"

I gave an annoyed shrug. "All I know is that my great-grandmother came from Tarbet. I only found out about it yesterday. I can't imagine that's a coincidence."

Alex's aunt nodded slowly. "Davina Boyle, your great-grandmother, was born and raised in Tarbet. She emigrated to the United States because she wanted to escape her gift. To her, it was a curse. She'd heard that if she moved far away from the home of her ancestors and her coven her abilities would slowly fade away. So she ran off to the other side of the world. I tried to stay in contact, to make sure she and her daughter, Kirsty, were all right. But then Kirsty's daughter—your mother—disappeared from my radar. I couldn't track her down until recently. A mutual relative contacted me when she was searching for her ancestors on a heritage website."

At that moment, the server brought us our dessert.

Mrs. MacDonald thanked her and dipped her spoon

into the creamy mixture dripping with red raspberry compote.

I just stared at the cranachan in front of me. There were too many conflicting thoughts in my head to focus on eating.

I was sure that Beatrice had to be the relative who had helped Mrs. MacDonald track my mom and me down. It was from Bea my mother had found out about our connection to Tarbet, after all.

At the same time, my brain tried to figure out how old Mrs. MacDonald was if she'd known my great-grandmother. I gave up after some complicated math had my head scrambled even more.

I remembered Alex had mentioned he called Mrs. MacDonald his aunt, even though she was a relative several times removed.

The main thing I was confused about was the gift Mrs. MacDonald had mentioned. Or the curse. And had she really mentioned a coven? Did that mean the same thing in Scotland as it did in the US? Maybe I'd merely misunderstood because of her accent.

But then, there *was* something that ran in the family, and it could be described as a curse.

"Was the thing Davina was trying to run away from her mental illness?" I asked, after Mrs. MacDonald had enjoyed her dessert in silence for a while. "Although you called it a gift, and surely that's not an apt description…"

Mrs. MacDonald put down her spoon. "Yes, I'm very saddened that your grandmother ended up in a psychiatric hospital because she had no support. I must assume Davina really managed to suppress her abilities, and she taught Kirsty the same. But some of us are more gifted than others, and in Kirsty, her abilities ran strong. She couldn't just ignore it. It's a crime, really. Do you know what your grandmother's supposed symptoms were? Or are?"

I frowned. "I don't know what she was diagnosed with, exactly. I always assumed she's schizophrenic, or psychotic maybe? I don't know that much about mental illness. Mom said Kirsty talked to imaginary people. Umm..." I rummaged around in my distant memory of the few times in the past my mother had even mentioned it. "I think she claimed she was seeing...ghosts?"

Mrs. MacDonald nodded gravely. "Bethany, your grandmother wasn't imagining anything. She isn't paranoid, and she certainly isn't ill. Like your great-grandmother and many of her female ancestors before that, Kirsty inherited the gift of communicating with spirits. There are a few other families in Tarbet with similar gifts. None of them can see ghosts, but women from those families have other magical talents. One has an affinity for herbs. Another has visions. One woman can see scenes that happened in the past. They're witches. I'm their leader. And you belong to this coven, Bethany, like your great-grandmother once did. You're a witch too."

I stared at this odd woman, trying to process what she was saying.

Then I looked around.

The other people in the restaurant were calmly eating their lunch.

The server rushed around to fill everyone's orders.

Alex was nowhere to be seen.

My eyes searched the ceiling beams, the tartan decorations, and the Highland Coo photographs for hidden cameras, but I couldn't spot anything like that.

Still, this had to be some kind of elaborate prank.

Everything I'd experienced since I'd arrived here had been odd, starting with Alex's behavior. He'd claimed he'd never wanted to give me the impression he was the wealthy owner of a castle, but had it really been on me that everything turned out to be so different from what I'd expected?

He'd been hot and cold toward me, and I'd had this feeling from the beginning of being gaslighted. Then there was the odd encounter with Euan Campbell at the castle. His getup had seemed like a costume to me. Why would he have played a prank on me? I wouldn't have even entertained the idea that it was a prank until Alex put it in my head, leading me to question everything. And then the alleged Euan hadn't turned up—again, I had to ask myself what a prankster would have gotten out of it—I had been scared out of my wits, and Alex had turned up as a convenient savior.

And now this.

Mrs. MacDonald, or whoever she really was, had seemed to be dressed up in a costume from the start. Most likely because she was playing some sort of bizarre role. Oh yeah, the part of a witch coven leader.

The whole thing had to be a setup for a TV show or something. My mother had to be in on the act, telling me about relatives in Tarbet. Maybe my great-grandmother wasn't even from Scotland! It was very unlike my mom to be involved with something as silly as this, but it was the only explanation…

Unless there really was a Tarbet connection, and this TV crew was exploiting it…

"This isn't a joke, Bethany," the old woman said, as if she could read my mind.

A strange sound escaped my throat—something like strangled laughter. "But that's… I mean…"

"I have tried many things to lure your mother to Scotland. Nothing worked. So I moved on to you. I found out you subscribed to the art magazine and that you were looking for a job. I placed the ad, hoping it would get your attention…and it worked. Of course, I did use a little magic to help my plan along." She gave a wry smile.

I suddenly remembered that my mother had been notified a while ago about winning a trip to Scotland. Mom never took part in competitions where you could win something like that, so she'd known it had to be a scam.

I decided to keep my cool, considering that I'd already lost it in previous footage and made a complete fool of myself. Although—surely there had to be a way to stop this TV show from ever airing. I had never signed a release form for anything like that, and I was reasonably sure nothing in my employment contract could be misconstrued as consent to appear in this prank show. One of my friends from college was engaged to a lawyer, and I resolved to ask him about it.

"Well, even if any of this were true," I said slowly, holding my composure. "I'm afraid I have to disappoint you. I've never seen a ghost in my life. And anyway, why exactly did you bring me here? To get the descendants of Davina Boyle to join your weird cult? That will not happen."

My raspberry cranachan had long since melted to a white and pink puddle. Meringue pieces floated around in it.

I stirred the mixture with a spoon, just to keep myself anchored to my seat. Otherwise, I would have stormed out of the restaurant. I couldn't wait to confront Alex.

But I was a little curious about what "Mrs. MacDonald" had to say.

What sort of story was she trying to spin?

I had to give it to the old broad—or maybe young actress in make-up? She was staying in character.

Her face was completely serious when she said, "I hoped your abilities were at least latent. I would have heard if they had been as strong as your grandmother's. But I assumed that coming back home, back to your roots, to the land of your ancestors, would make them more pronounced. Here, you'd have the coven as a support system. And, to tell you the truth, we need a Boyle descendant in our midst. I'm clairvoyant, and I've seen that we could really use your gift soon."

I mentally applauded the scriptwriters of this little prank show. It was all very well done, and above all, intriguing.

"Like I said." I tried to keep my voice even. "I have to disappoint you. I don't have this…gift. If I could see ghosts in Scotland, I'm sure I would have noticed by now."

Suddenly, Alex's voice rang out behind me.

"Didn't you have a very vivid encounter with the ghost of Euan Campbell only yesterday?"

CHAPTER ELEVEN

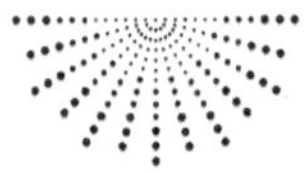

I froze.

Alex didn't notice my reaction. He sat back down in his chair. "I'm only joking. Bethany met someone at the castle yesterday who pretended to be Euan Campbell. He asked her out on a date. I told her someone was pulling a prank—or it was a ghost."

Now Alex must have seen my face, because his jovial tone changed. "Oh, I'm sorry. Not that funny. I don't know why I was making a joke out of it. We don't know what this person's intention was, and he didn't turn up for the date at the castle. Bethany was terrified."

He looked down at my uneaten dessert. "Is something wrong? Did the food not agree with you? Or is it really because of what I said? I apologize!"

"Don't worry, Alex," Mrs. MacDonald said. She leaned forward and asked me, "What was it like? Your encounter with Euan Campbell?"

I didn't say a word.

When the silence dragged on, Alex nervously spoke. "Umm, no, you must have misunderstood, Aunt Mary. Bethany didn't really see a ghost. At least not during the day. She spoke to the impostor and everything. Although you had a funny experience in the castle that evening too, didn't you, Bethany?"

I kept quiet, and he touched my hand. "You're not still upset about that, are you? We did say your imagination went haywire and the atmosphere in that old castle…"

"It wasn't her imagination, Alex," Mrs. MacDonald interrupted.

I scooted my chair back, which made a loud, screechy noise on the tiles. I winced. "Excuse me," I got out.

Grabbing my phone out of my purse, I got up to run outside.

I paced on the lawn outside the restaurant until my mother finally picked up the phone.

"Hello?" she answered in a sleepy voice.

I'd completely forgotten about the time difference. Well, I'd already woken her up now, and this was important.

"Hi, Mom, it's Beth. Did Beatrice tell you my great-grandmother's name? You know, the one who emigrated from Tarbet?"

"What? Honey, I was fast asleep…"

"I'm sorry I woke you, Mom, but this is really important. I'm in Tarbet right now, and I need to know."

"Umm…All right. Wait, I wrote it down." I heard a rustling sound and imagined her going through the clutter on her desk. My mom was a neat freak and terribly well organized, but strangely, her desk, where she did all the organizing, was always a mess.

Just when I thought I couldn't possibly stand it any longer, she said, "Ah, yes. Boyle. Her name was Davina Boyle."

I suddenly felt dizzy.

Slowly, I sat down on the edge of a flower box.

"Mom?" I couldn't help it, but my voice sounded like that of a little girl. "Have you ever seen a ghost?"

There was a deafening silence. It felt like a bomb had gone off. That's how charged the atmosphere through the phone line was.

"Mom, I know Grandma sees ghosts. That's what you said, right? That's the reason she was diagnosed with a mental illness. Have you ever…or did you think you saw—"

"Oh god. Listen to me, honey." My mother's voice suddenly sounded very awake. "I've been watching for signs of this your whole life, but I thought you were spared. I didn't want to burden you. But since you're asking about it, I have to assume… Well, it happened to me when I was younger. I told no one after what they did to my mother. The good news is that I got rid of it all by myself, and I'm sure you can too. You just have to ignore it. Trust me. If you think someone who isn't really there is speaking to you, don't give them any attention. In time, this will go away. I promise!"

I was so shocked, I couldn't say anything.

"Beth? Are you still there?"

"Yes. Yes, Mom." I swallowed. "Um, thanks. That… cleared up a lot. Thank you."

"Are you sure? Maybe you should come home."

"No, it's okay. I'm all right."

"If you're sure… Call me if you need to, and I'll walk you through it again. Anytime, okay?"

"Okay, Mom. Don't worry about me. I have to hang up now. Talk to you later."

I felt numb as I pressed the red button on the phone and walked back inside the restaurant.

I didn't say anything to Alex and his aunt when I sat back down, even though they looked at me expectantly.

Had Mrs. MacDonald told Alex everything? Did he

believe in ghosts and witches? The impression he'd given me so far was that he didn't.

As if she had read my thoughts, Mrs. MacDonald glanced at Alex and gave a tiny shake of her head.

"Listen, Bethany, I just told Alex that I'd love for you to meet a few young women from Tarbet. They're all members of the local women's club, which I chair, and we happen to be having a meeting tonight. He said he could spare you for one evening. I have a small B&B, and you can have one of the guest rooms there. What do you say?"

Agreeing to this would be the complete opposite of what my mother had just advised. I should really go back to Alex's cottage. The best plan would be to avoid the castle entirely—any old buildings, really.

I feared what this "women's club" would do to me. Would they brainwash me into believing in ghosts and witches and all that?

But then, I already kind of knew that they didn't need to. Ghosts either existed or they didn't, and my own mother had as much as admitted to the fact that they did. I wasn't quite ready to admit that the person I'd interacted with on the castle grounds had been dead Sir Euan Campbell.

I couldn't deny, though, that I'd experienced strange phenomena that fell into the realm of the paranormal—and clearly other women in my family had experienced the same.

One of my options was to run away from it, hide, and suppress it, like Davina and my mother. But if I wasn't successful, I could end up like my grandmother.

Or I could confront it, deal with it head-on.

Honestly, I didn't feel like I had much of a choice at all.

I felt like Alice, who'd tumbled down the rabbit hole. I had to face the surreal, nonsensical world on the other side.

"Okay, I'll stay," I said with a brittle voice. "I'll meet the women from your…club."

CHAPTER TWELVE

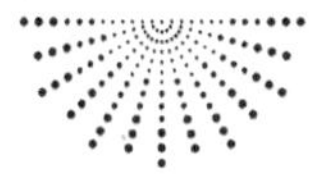

Once Alex had taken his leave, Mrs. MacDonald and I walked to Tarbet.

She carried a walking stick but seemed surprisingly spry for her age.

We stopped at a local shop where I bought a toothbrush, toothpaste, and make-up-remover wipes. The shop was really just a post office with a few extra shelves where you could get the most basic supplies, but somehow they had everything I needed for an impromptu overnight stay.

Well, except for clean underwear and PJs, but Mrs. MacDonald reassured me she'd organize sleepwear for me. I'd just have to go home tomorrow in the same clothes I'd worn today. Luckily, I always carried a small make-up bag in my purse, so at least I wouldn't have to worry about Alex seeing me without "my face" on tomorrow.

One advantage of having to go to the Tarbet shop was that it was located close to the pier. So at least I got to see Loch Lomond, after all. It really was beautiful, surrounded by the mountains. On this bright summer day, even the tops were visible, so I got to enjoy the scenery in all its glory.

We took a walk along the shore of Loch Lomond without talking much. I was glad Mrs. MacDonald didn't pressure me into discussing what she'd told me. I needed to think about a few things before I felt ready for that.

We took a turn away from the loch, along a footpath, and across some meadows, and I thought we were walking toward the main road that connected Tarbet and Arrochar. We never got to it, though. Instead, we ended up in front of a beautifully restored old cottage. It had whitewashed walls, a thatched roof, and pink climbing roses, and it was surrounded by lush foliage. It looked like a postcard.

We knocked, and the most gorgeous-looking woman I'd ever seen in real life opened the door. She was tall, with wavy blond hair and catlike green eyes.

Mrs. MacDonald introduced her as Penny Reid.

"Our meeting tonight is taking place at Penny's house," she explained.

I was quite intimidated by Penny and her home, so I just nodded.

I soon warmed toward the blond woman, however, after she'd led us to the kitchen and served us coffee and delicious homemade brownies.

Penny showed me her bedroom upstairs, where we found a T-shirt and shorts for me to wear as PJs.

Then Penny opened the door to another room. "This is the guest room I told you about earlier."

As far as I understood it, Penny had had a roommate who'd had a baby and recently moved out.

"You're welcome to stay here tonight. Might be more comfortable than the Thistle Inn."

Penny's comment could have been completely innocent, but I had been worried about what Mrs. MacDonald's B&B would be like, hoping it wouldn't match the appearance of its owner.

I took one look at the queen-size bed with crisp white

linen and the minimalistic but tasteful decor and gladly agreed to stay there.

Back downstairs, Mrs. MacDonald was already at the front door, informing us she would pop back home and get a ride with one of the other women to come back that evening. She didn't seem offended or even surprised when I told her I'd stay at Penny's. She just smiled in a peculiar manner—as if she'd already known it would happen.

We had another cup of coffee, and then Penny gave me a tour of her very impressive garden. There were sections with herbs and others with flowers, broken up by a meadow and a little pond. I liked the rose garden best, with meandering paths between rows and rows of sweet-smelling pink and red roses.

Penny had her own business, selling cosmetics and other products like candles that were made from her herbs and flowers. "I use rose petals a lot," Penny explained.

She gave me a sideways glance when she added, "Aside from the herbal ingredients, I put in a little something that makes my products extra special. Magic."

I must have flinched, because she patted my back. "This is new to you, I know, but we have to talk about it sometime. And you're going to see some wild things tonight when the other witches demonstrate their abilities. So showing you a little herbal magic is easing you in."

I fingered a rose petal, not daring to look at Penny. My throat was tight, but I got out, "So, you're an herb witch, then?"

"Yes."

"What do you do, exactly?" I glanced at her, then looked back at the roses.

"I used to do all sorts of things. Most spells require herbs, and I have a particular knack for love potions and beauty potions...hence the roses. But I don't do much of that anymore. I've made some big mistakes in the past and changed my ways…"

I looked at her, intrigued. Before I could ask what she meant by that, Penny continued with a twinkle in her eyes. "I still do beauty products. They work particularly well, thanks to my herbal magic. But I've recently gotten into healing with herbs too."

No matter how conflicted I felt about the whole thing, I couldn't resist asking about her cosmetic products. If she used them herself and looked like that as a result, she'd definitely convert me.

When asked, Penny laughed. "Yes, I do use them myself. I used to put a lot of time and effort into making myself look very beautiful. But I have to credit my good genes too."

"Oh," I said, a little crestfallen.

"You don't need to worry about that," Penny said, waving her hand. "You're so young and pretty, with that flawless skin and gorgeous auburn hair."

It reminded me of what Alex had said, that I was just a boring pretty girl.

Penny must have read my facial expression. "Do you have self-esteem issues? Believe me, beauty products—or spells—won't fix that. It's like with cosmetic surgery addiction."

"It's not that. I've always felt confident about my looks. I know I'm pretty. But a certain someone thinks I'm not special enough." I shrugged.

"Really?" Penny raised an eyebrow. "Well, if he's looking for something special in the way you look, then that's the problem right there. Maybe he'd find something truly special if he'd look further than skin deep."

"You're right. He should look at what's below the surface," I concurred, my mood lightening. "That's his job." Suddenly I had an idea about how I could assist Alex. I'd help him see the beauty in everyday things and activities again so that he could better envision the beautiful form inside a hunk of stone. "You've really given me a great idea," I said to Penny.

She laughed. "I don't know what you're talking about, but I'm glad. Do you want to see how I make my products?"

"Definitely! Maybe I could sample some of them?"

"That could be arranged."

Penny led me to a garden hut. There was a workspace outside. It featured a fireplace and a big cauldron. My mind immediately went to witches, but I still couldn't quite grasp that Penny was supposed to be one.

I definitely couldn't believe that *I* was supposed to be one.

The inside of the hut was more spacious and lighter than I would have guessed from the outside. There was a large table with some lavender sprigs spread across it.

More lavender and other herbs were bunched together and hung from the ceiling to dry.

It smelled so good inside the hut—of lavender and chamomile and other herbs I couldn't identify.

Penny poured a bit of the lavender and chamomile bath salt she'd freshly made into a glass for me.

Meanwhile, I perused the contents of a large cabinet. There were small apothecary bottles, larger green bottles, and glass jars full of all sorts of herbal products. A rose facial cream caught my eye, and I asked Penny if I could sample that too.

"I used to buy this organic rose facial cream that was fantastic, but it's been discontinued."

"Sure," Penny said. "If you open the cabinet doors at the bottom, you'll find spare cream jars."

I bent down and spotted some in the back. I reached

in, and my fingers touched an old book. It felt like I received an electric shock.

"Ouch." I pulled my hand back.

"What happened?" Penny asked with concern. "Did you cut yourself on something?"

"No…" I carefully reached back inside the cabinet and pulled the book out, this time prepared for the sharp sting.

"It's this book. I get that sometimes, with old things and furniture…" I told Penny about my love for antiques, my studies, and my career aspirations. "I'm used to feeling something…like a little tingling sensation. Nothing as strong as this just now. Umm, I always thought that it meant I had a special connection to antiques…"

"You do!" Penny laughed. "A very special connection. And it makes sense that your ability has gotten stronger since you came here. Mrs. MacDonald told me about your family and how your great-grandmother tried to let her gift fade by moving far away. Sounds like you have always had latent abilities, Beth, but now that you're here, with your coven, your gift is really emerging. Let's see what you have there."

"Oh…" I straightened up, the book in my hand.

Penny took it from me. "Ah, yes, it's a grimoire."

My eyes widened. "A grimoire?" I thought about horror movies where witch books caused all kinds of evil things to happen. I involuntarily took a step back.

"Of sorts. My ancestors wrote down how they helped people with herbs, noting magic and spells in code. Ever since the witch hunts, women with special gifts have been much more careful about writing incriminating evidence down. Still, they wanted to record their work for themselves and for their daughters. I'm just really thankful that something survived."

She held up the little leather-bound journal. "It makes sense that this would cause a powerful reaction if you can sense energy from people who have handled items in the past. It's a form of psychometry, but with you it probably comes from your ability to see ghosts—their residual energy from the past that has survived too."

"I guess," I said skeptically. "I never thought about it like that before. But…that wouldn't be so bad. If that's my main…ability, I mean."

I brightened up a little, for the first time more positive about the whole unbelievable story Mrs. MacDonald had sprung on me.

I already loved antiques and the stories attached to them. They've always been more than soulless material objects to me. It was kind of neat to think I was feeling the energy of the people who'd touched precious old items before me, imbuing the items with meaning, giving them a life of their own.

"It sounds like you aren't that comfortable with the full extent of your ability," Penny said. "Communicating with ghosts?"

My mood instantly darkened again. "I don't know. That's what Mrs. MacDonald claims I can do, anyway. My grandmother said she can see ghosts, and she ended up being committed. My mother grew up in a foster family."

"Oh, I'm so sorry, Bethany. That's tough. If only your great-grandmother hadn't left Tarbet and the coven. Then maybe your grandmother and your mother could have thrived instead of suffered."

"Hmm. I wouldn't have been born then, though. And my mother had a good life. She ended up in a loving family. She managed to somehow…suppress…this talent… I guess. And she seems happy, so…" I shrugged.

"Is she? It must take a lot of energy and effort to repress such an essential part of herself. And I imagine she always feels as if something vital is missing." Penny said this as an offhand comment as she put some of the rose cream in the jar I had finally retrieved from the cupboard.

It really struck a chord with me, though. What she said about Mom was so true. I'd always thought it was because of her childhood trauma and the missing connection to her mother—but what if it was more than that?

I knew it would be difficult to talk to Mom about it, especially since I wasn't really sure I believed everything Mrs. MacDonald had said about my family "gift."

I did become a believer that night, though, at least where the existence of witches and magic was concerned.

How could I not?

At least a dozen women demonstrated things that couldn't be explained by the laws of physics and left me completely mind-blown.

While the jury was still out on the effect of Penny's beauty products, the herb witch had made a flower bloom right in front of my eyes.

A young weather witch named Jem flew into the air on her stave.

Someone conjured up a scene from the past right there, in Penny's garden.

A red-haired, full-figured woman who was about Jem's age, Fionna, asked me to pick a scene from a book. Then she spelled the book, and she made the scene come alive on the TV screen.

As we sat around the fire pit in Penny's garden, other witches told me about their abilities. Tales of visions, soothsaying, elemental magic, astral projection, and much more. I had no idea if they were true or not, but after a couple of glasses of wine, I was ready to believe everything...especially after what I'd already witnessed.

And I was definitely ready to believe in this special community, this coven. I finally felt like I had arrived somewhere, like I belonged.

It was a great night.

The next day, I was feeling the effects of the hangover, though.

On the train ride home, doubts crept in.

The coven *was* great. Witches did exist, and what a great and safe space for them to practice Tarbet's "women's club" was.

But did I really belong among them?

Apart from feeling a bit of a zing when I touched old things, what proof did I even have that I'd inherited my great-grandmother's ability?

I only vaguely remembered Grandma Kirsty claiming to see ghosts. What if she had just been mentally ill after all?

Did I really think I'd seen the ghost of Euan Campbell in front of the castle the other day?

I'd never seen the vaguest of specters before, and then I travel to Scotland, and, boom, I see a ghost who seems so real to me I can't distinguish him from a person made of flesh and blood?

It seemed unlikely.

Then another thought occurred to me. What if I'd seen ghosts before and I hadn't known it?

I looked around the train compartment. There was an older man in old-fashioned clothes reading a newspaper. He was noisy, rustling the pages, coughing loudly, but nobody ever looked his way.

Maybe because he was invisible, and nobody saw him but me.

Was that possible?

I shook my head, as if trying to shake off the preposterous idea, but I kept glancing over at the old man.

A little later, someone asked the man to move his briefcase so he could take a seat next to him.

Not a ghost, then.

Relieved, I sank a little deeper into my seat.

My head hurt, and I was exhausted.

I was probably driving myself crazy, thinking about all of this now.

I closed my eyes and fell asleep, only waking when the train conductor announced we'd arrived at the last station, Oban.

I rubbed my eyes. Now everything that had happened the night before felt even more like a dream.

A knock against the window made me wince.

It was Alex, smiling and pointing at the door.

I nodded and rushed to get off.

"Hi," Alex greeted me. "Did you fall asleep on the train?"

I just nodded.

"Quite a night, was it?" he teased.

"Oh, you have no idea."

CHAPTER THIRTEEN

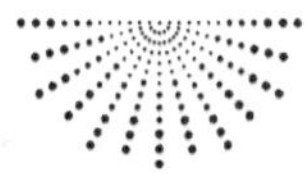

Once we got home, I had a shower and changed, then puttered around the cottage before deciding to take another nap.

Afterward, I went for a walk—in the opposite direction of the castle—and when I got back, I offered to cook dinner.

I made my signature dish, spaghetti with tomato sauce, and if Alex had had more exciting and flavorful meals, he was polite enough not to mention it.

While we were eating, I fielded Alex's questions about my time in Tarbet.

"It was nice to meet everyone." I tried to stay vague and then changed the subject. "Unfortunately, I didn't get to ask your aunt about the history of the castle, and I'd love to know more about it. Maybe you can fill me in?"

"Hmm." Alex swallowed his forkful of spaghetti. "What do you want to know?"

"Everything!" I smiled. "I'm a history buff, so you can't bore me."

"No, but I could bore myself." Alex grinned. "But, okay, I'll tell you what I know. Invercreran Castle was built in the early seventeenth century by Sir Duncan Campbell, who went down in history as Black Duncan. The Campbell clan later moved on, and the castle stood empty for a while. Euan Campbell's father restored it at the end of the nineteenth century. The family resided here. Euan was an only child. After his parents passed, he lived in the castle by himself."

"Did he not have a family of his own?"

Alex shook his head. "He never got married. Rumor has it he was a bit of a Casanova. Supposedly, he entertained a different woman at the castle every night."

I raised my eyebrows.

Alex laughed. "These sorts of stories tend to get wilder with every reiteration. But there must have been some truth to it. Euan loved beautiful women. And they say it was his undoing, in the end."

I leaned forward, my dinner forgotten, now completely captivated by the story. "Was he killed by a woman? Out of jealousy? Or revenge?"

"Oh no, not that." Alex laughed. "His heart gave out. It must have been one exciting night too many. One of his staff found him dead in his bed the next morning. He looked asleep—as if he was having a pleasant dream, in fact. Apparently, he had a smile on his face. Esme MacDonald, the maid, disappeared that same night. Not surprisingly, gossip is that Esme had been the woman who had made Euan's heart a little too happy, if you know what I mean." Alex winked.

"MacDonald? Like your aunt?" My voice was squeaky with excitement. Alex didn't seem to notice, because he shoved more food into his mouth.

"Hmmm," he said, before swallowing. "Aunt Mary's mother. Evidently, she must have been pregnant with Mary at the time. Hence the rumors."

"But...you said she disappeared, ran away in shock,

when Euan collapsed during lovemaking? She must have come back and presented her daughter as Euan's child for your Aunt Mary to inherit the castle, no?"

"Esme did reappear, but as a fortune-teller in a circus. That's where Aunt Mary grew up, among the Travellers. Mary later moved in with her grandmother in Tarbet."

"Okay…" So I could actually do the math and answer the question of how old Mrs. MacDonald was, if I found out Euan's date of death.

"Esme didn't come back here, though. She never tried to pass off Mary as Euan's child. Many years later, Mary turned up and claimed to be Euan's daughter. It was a difficult situation because there had been many disputes over the rightful inheritance of the castle. After Euan's death, it stood empty. Nobody could do anything with it, or its contents, because the legal battles just dragged on. And then comes Mary—this was in the sixties—who claims to be Sir Euan's daughter. She was a respectable inhabitant of Tarbet by that time, but it was an open secret that she grew up with the Travellers. You can imagine the scandal this caused in the Campbell family. A 'gypsy' woman claiming to be a Campbell."

"Couldn't they just ignore her and continue with their own fight for the estate? Mrs. MacDonald couldn't have proven her relationship to Euan Campbell, so her claim could hardly be substantiated."

Alex took a piece of bread and wiped up the sauce from his plate. "I think there were documents that gave her claim some credence. There was another problem, though. You mustn't forget, there had been a lot going on in the world since Euan Campbell's death. The Great Depression, then World War II. All this time, the castle had been left to rot. And the Campbells had other problems. Most of them were broke. Nobody would have been able to restore the castle or take care of the estate. But they were like dogs with a bone. They didn't want to let it go. The castle sort of represented what the Campbell clan had stood for, once upon a time, so... Anyway, Mary just bided her time, quietly collecting evidence. If I recall correctly, there was a letter that proved the affair and Euan's promise to marry Esme. In any case, in the nineties, there was the possibility of DNA evidence. And that finally settled the dispute."

"Oh, so that must have made the Campbells angry."

"Funnily enough, by that time, nobody really cared anymore. Not about the castle, at least. The surrounding land was worth quite a bit of money and provided more of an opportunity. So when Aunt Mary suggested forming a trust for the heirs and they came to an agreement about the land, everyone was relieved more than anything. I'm part of that trust too. We all benefit from the rent collected through land leases. Mary owns the castle and this cottage, though, and she is kind enough to let me live here."

I dug back into my pasta, but it was cold by now.

"So she's owned the castle for thirty years? Why hasn't she done anything with it?"

Alex shrugged. "The renovation would cost a lot of money. She probably doesn't have it."

"It's odd that she went through so much trouble to get it and then just left it like it is, though."

"I guess she just wanted to have her rightful inheritance. And...well...maybe there's another explanation. The castle is... Let's just say people avoid it. Like it's cursed. I can believe that my aunt puts stock in such things."

"You mean, it's haunted?"

I held my breath as I waited for his answer.

Alex swayed his head back and forth. "People say it's haunted. If you believe in ghosts. But there certainly is a negative energy in there. Even I can feel that. I don't like to go in there either. I mean, you know what I'm talking about. You felt it the other night, right?"

I didn't want to go into that with Alex, so I took a sip of water.

"Scottish castles are supposed to be haunted," I said in a light tone. "And it's no surprise people think that about Invercreran, if its last inhabitant died there before his time and under such scandalous circumstances."

I refilled my glass from the carafe on the table. "Speaking of which, did nobody think his death was a little suspicious? If Sir Euan was young and otherwise healthy, did nobody suspect foul play?"

I didn't know that much about the whole ghost thing, but it didn't seem likely that someone who died from natural causes and with no trauma would still haunt the castle after all these years.

"I don't think they found any evidence of that. The way it's told, Sir Euan lay on his bed, dressed up in his Campbell kilt. It looked as if he was sleeping peacefully."

I had a sudden image of Euan Campbell lying asleep on his bed—it was the four-poster bed with red-and-gold jacquard fabric I'd "seen" at the castle. Somehow my mind mixed this up with the pink climbing roses that trailed up our cottage.

They reminded me of Sleeping Beauty.

The image sent shivers down my spine.

It didn't really make sense at all. Euan Campbell was clearly dead, not some fairy-tale character who had been asleep for a hundred years and could be awakened with a kiss.

But somehow I couldn't get rid of the idea.

I pushed my plate away.

"Are you all right?" Alex asked, glancing at the food on my plate. "You've hardly eaten anything. Your cooking isn't that bad."

I smiled at his joke. "No, it's fine. I'm just not that hungry. To be honest, I overdid it a little yesterday. Indulged in too much wine and food. My stomach still doesn't feel that great. I might make myself an herbal tea and go to bed early."

"Of course. Here, let me clean up." Alex stacked my plate on his.

"If you're sure…"

"You already did the cooking, so this is my job. You go ahead and make your tea."

"Thanks." I got up to put the kettle on the stove and grabbed a mug from the Welsh dresser.

"I have one more question about Euan Campbell," I said in a very by-the-way tone. "Where's he buried?"

"All the Campbells are buried in the small family graveyard behind the castle." Alex stopped in his tracks. "Euan must have been the last, of course. I'm not sure if I've seen his name on a gravestone. But he's probably there." He continued with the dishes.

I just nodded, choosing a bag of chamomile tea from the herbal infusion selection. When the water boiled, I poured some into my mug and then said goodnight to Alex.

In my room, I drank my tea, but I couldn't go to sleep.

I just lay in my bed thinking about everything for hours.

It was clear to me that Mrs. MacDonald had brought me to Scotland to contact Euan Campbell's ghost. She wanted me to help him find peace, move on, so the castle would finally be free of him. The Tarbet coven leader probably hoped that this would get me to embrace my gift fully, so that I and my family eventually returned to the coven.

At least I assumed that's what people who had my gift

usually did…get the ghost to move on. That's what they did in books and on TV.

But there was no way I was ready for that. I'd only just discovered my strange ability. I had no idea how it worked, what I could see, what I could do…

And as friendly and helpful as the young witches of the coven had been, none of them had my ability, so none could give me guidance.

The only people who could have done so, the women in my family, had either repressed their gift or had misinterpreted it as something that needed to be treated with strong medication.

I felt very much alone.

Still, the only other option would be to turn away from everything I'd learned in the last few days and return home. Maybe distance from the Old World and my roots would help, and the abilities that had started to bloom in Scotland would go away again.

But to be sure, I'd have to cut myself off from the slightest possibility of encountering a ghost again. Live in a brand-new building, avoid going out as much as possible. I certainly couldn't work with antique furniture. In fact, my whole art history degree would have been for nothing. The past, and any items that could still have the energy of someone who touched it in the past, would be off limits.

I would have to start from scratch, always looking over my shoulder, always on the run from ghosts.

I didn't want a life like that.

I didn't want to give up everything that was dear to me.

I didn't want to give myself up.

And I realized it was part of me, whatever this was.

I was a witch who could see ghosts, whether or not I wanted to accept it.

Sighing, I tossed and turned in my bed.

Really, I had no choice but to face Euan Campbell.

I had to go back to that castle, feel all the strange feelings, and see the disturbing images that being there invoked in me.

Somehow, I had to make Euan understand that he had been dead for a hundred years.

I could only hope he'd see the light.

If that even existed.

Or there was no telling what would happen.

To him. To me.

I was in completely uncharted territory here.

I was literally scared to death.

And I had no idea who the Bethany would be who'd come out on the other side of this.

Cold laughter bubbled up inside of me, and I pressed my face into the pillow to stop myself from becoming hysterical.

I'd dreamed about a life-changing experience on my way over to Scotland for my new job.

This wasn't exactly what I'd imagined.

CHAPTER FOURTEEN

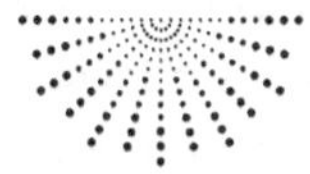

By the time the moon was glowing in the dark sky, I had made up my mind.

I dressed up in the same outfit I'd picked two nights ago for my date with Euan.

Then I quietly crept to the bathroom, putting on make-up and styling my hair.

Once I was ready, I tiptoed past Alex's room to the kitchen. I really didn't want him to wake up. Having him as a rescue option was nice, but I had to do this by myself, and a knight in shining armor would only prevent me from seeing it through.

In the kitchen, I found a flashlight and put it in a tote bag. I also put the key for the castle in there. I left through the back via Alex's workshop so I didn't have to go past his room again.

The stone sculptures stood like guards in the semi-darkness and made my heart flutter. I quickly exited the workshop and made my way through the garden.

I didn't need the flashlight since there were almost no clouds in the sky and the moonlight illuminated the path to the castle.

I took a few deep breaths before I pushed open the heavy iron gate, then marched straight to the entrance door.

My fingers shook a little when I got the key out of the tote bag and stuck it in the lock.

It turned smoothly, and I switched on my flashlight before pushing the door open and stepping inside.

I flinched when the door closed behind me with a heavy thud, then walked into the foyer.

My flashlight beam danced over the sheet-covered furniture. I walked to the old Chesterfield sofa and pulled off the sheet. Bending over to examine the details more closely, I was pleased to find that it was indeed an original.

I recognized the beechwood frame, the brown leather in classic Chesterfield pleats, and symmetrically arranged leather buttons. It was in need of repair, but once restored, it might be quite valuable.

I uncovered two more pieces of furniture: a well-preserved two-seater and an armchair, which completed the Chesterfield suite.

If my find was any indication of what other antique treasures might be hidden in this castle, a fortune had been rotting away here for decades.

This gave me even more of an incentive to face the ghost that was haunting this castle.

Even though I had no idea how to banish him—or help him move on, or whatever witches with my gift did—I imagined my success would constitute a good bargaining chip.

I wanted to persuade Mrs. MacDonald to give me the job of overseeing the restoration and sale of the furniture in this castle.

Being a muse was all well and good, but it wasn't actually a full-time job. And this was what I'd been working toward in my studies, what I was really interested in.

Even though I would have liked to see what else was under the sheets in the big hall, I followed the call that I'd heard last time, which I'd managed to ignore thus far.

Once I paid attention to it, though, it was quite insistent.

I walked up the stairs, through the salon with the taxidermied animals, and ascended the iron spiral staircase up the little tower.

I noticed my red clutch on one of the steps, but I didn't even stop to retrieve it.

As I stood in front of the oak door, the same vivid image of the room's interior returned. I was pulled into the vortex of conflicting emotions when the man appeared, ready to seduce me.

I desperately wanted to give in to his call. But it felt like I had been socialized not to. I had been taught to repress it —even though nobody had ever named what it was that I was burying deep inside me.

In order to overcome my conditioning, I had to tap into something bigger than myself, something that reached beyond my twenty-three years. Some sort of collective consciousness of all the women who'd come before me, the ancestors who had been given this gift.

Many of them might have had the support of female relatives, but they were still fighting against the efforts of a patriarchal society that was afraid of women with intuitive abilities. They all had stepped into their power, and now I had to too.

I imagined all of them standing there with me, at the top of this staircase.

I could feel how this moment in front of the door was pregnant with the potential for transformation. If I heeded the call, I'd never be the same. And this wasn't just about my career or what I was going to do with my life.

It was about who I was, at my core.

A witch.

I turned the doorknob and entered the tower room.

CHAPTER FIFTEEN

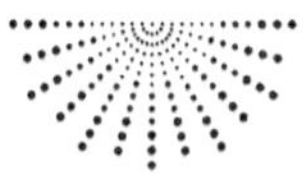

The scent of pink roses enveloped me.

I blinked and took a moment to get my bearings.

It did not surprise me, really, that the room looked exactly as I had imagined it. The large four-poster mahogany bed with ornately carved bedposts. A red-and-gold canopy and a matching bedspread, all made of heavy jacquard.

Rose petals littered the bed and the floor, which must have been the reason for the powerful scent.

There was a washing table with a white ceramic bowl and matching pitcher. A mahogany bureau with lots of little drawers. An oriental carpet and matching drapes, all in red interwoven with golden threads. A card table with champagne flutes and dishes covered in silver cloches.

The room looked magnificent—not at all like the rest of the dilapidated castle. Yes, some of the furniture downstairs had held up remarkably well, but it was still marked by time. In here, it looked as if time hadn't passed at all.

None of the fabric was faded, and, most remarkably, there wasn't a speck of dusk anywhere.

My only explanation was that the ghost of Euan Campbell wielded its own kind of magic, preserving the room as it had been the day he'd died.

A soft piano tune filled the room, and when I took a few steps, I saw a gramophone on a low table on the other side of the bed.

Euan Campbell materialized out of thin air, suddenly standing in front of the window. He gave me quite a start, even though I really should have expected him.

My hand went to my heart.

"Bethany, my sweet muse. You came."

I forced a smile. "Sure."

"May I have this dance?"

He gave a little bow and came closer.

"Umm, I…"

Before I could think up an excuse for not being touched by a ghost, he already had his hand on my waist.

At least he tried to put it there. Instead, Euan's hand went straight through my dress, and it felt like being stabbed by an icicle. I shivered and felt goosebumps all over.

He didn't seem to notice, which bothered me for two reasons.

This could have been a good demonstration, proving to him he was a ghost.

Euan also didn't seem to have an awareness that his touch was having a negative effect on me. His insensitivity probably couldn't be explained away by his ghostliness but instead said more about his character.

After the initial shock of his icy touch subsided, I extricated myself from it and put a bit of distance between us.

Euan grimaced. "What's the matter? I'm not being too forward, am I?"

"No, that's not it, umm…" I stammered. "It's just that I heard rumors about you and…supposedly, you're already, um…betrothed to another. A woman named Esme?"

I clearly couldn't just confront him with the fact that he was dead and thus unable to touch me, so I hoped jogging his memory about his last days would gently steer him in the right direction.

"Oh. Yes, I was. But Esme left me. She just ran away."

He looked at me with big puppy-dog eyes, and if I hadn't known the truth about the circumstances, I would have felt sorry for him.

"She didn't just leave you, though, did she? They say she was with child, and you refused to do the honorable thing and marry her."

Euan seemed crestfallen. "That isn't true. Esme was my love."

My skepticism must have shown on my face because he continued. "Ordinarily, I don't speak of other women when I'm with someone. I'd like to give all my attention to you, sweet Bethany. But it seems as if my character has been called into question, and so I deem it necessary to defend myself. I cared for Esme very much. There's proof."

He went over to the bureau, attempting to open a drawer. He was more precise than when he attempted to place his hand on my waist, but he still didn't manage to open it.

To spare him some dignity, I said, "Your hands are shaking with indignation. Here, let me." I opened the drawer for him.

He nodded and stepped aside. "There's a small box, and in it is a golden key."

I found the box with assorted items like pins and coins and rummaged through them until I found a tiny key.

"If you slide your hand alongside the bureau halfway down, you'll notice a slight indentation. Press on it, and a secret compartment will open up."

I bent down to do so, and a hidden mechanism moved a wooden panel at the top so another drawer became visible. I inserted the key and turned it, then pulled the drawer out.

"I've kept all the little love tokens Esme has given me."

I stood on my toes to peer into the drawer. All I saw was a small glass jar.

I took it out. It appeared to be sealed with wax, and there was a dark brown substance in it. "There's only this."

Euan frowned. "No, there should be pressed flowers. Little drawings. She wasn't great with words, so I didn't get letters and poems like I wrote to her, but she was a gifted artist."

I put my hand in the drawer and felt around inside, but it was empty.

"Sorry, nothing else in here. Are you sure you didn't store them somewhere else?"

He came over to have a look himself. "Where else would I put those keepsakes than in my secret drawer?" When he was satisfied that I had been telling the truth, though, he seemed puzzled. "Hmm." He moved away from the bureau and paced the room.

"Did Esme take them before she left, perhaps?" He mused aloud. "She knew of the hidden compartment."

I put the small jar back and closed the drawer, not bothering to lock it again.

"Maybe she did." If Esme was responsible for Euan's death somehow, it would have made sense for her to remove all evidence of their love trysts.

Her love tokens, as Euan had called them, might have been hidden in the desk, but Euan didn't seem to be worried about keeping the hidden drawer a secret. He'd shown Esme, and now he'd told me about it… Esme could have been worried that others knew about the drawer as well.

If she wanted to remove herself from the suspect list in case Euan's death was treated as suspicious, she wouldn't have wanted to leave hard evidence of their love affair behind.

Euan drew different conclusions, though.

"She probably took everything to keep for herself, so she would remember our love. Her feelings for me were real, then. Why did she run?"

He really seemed puzzled, which I thought was interesting.

"Are you sure you didn't give her the impression you weren't going to marry her, after all? Miscommunication might be at fault. It often is. If she misunderstood you, she might have been so hurt that she didn't confront you about it but ran instead."

Euan made a face. "Why, yes. I never could have married her, despite my feelings. She was a maid, you see. A simple girl from a village. As much as I loved her, it wouldn't have been seemly. I would have married her in spirit, and that's what I'd promised her, really. She would have understood that."

I tried my best not to roll my eyes. "If she was with child, a marriage in spirit probably wouldn't have been enough for her. She needed someone to provide for her."

"Oh, I would have done that, Bethany," Euan protested. "I told her I'd look after her. She and the bairn would have wanted for nothing. But I couldn't make our union official. She'd always known that."

"As a woman, I can very well believe that she fervently hoped you'd change your mind about that. And that she was very disappointed when you didn't. Frankly, I understand she didn't want to be relegated to the role of mistress. She probably didn't want to share you either. Didn't you… carry on with other women…?" At the sight of his raised eyebrows, I held up my hands. "Just repeating what I've heard."

"I certainly was spending time with ladies. I'm not a social recluse. And it is my duty to find a suitable wife, my feelings for Esme regardless."

Now it was my turn to raise an eyebrow. "Is that why you asked me here tonight? Because you believe I could be a suitable wife? Surely not."

He gave me a charming smile. "Of course not, Bethany. You're not a wife, you are a muse. Much more exciting. And as much as I loved Esme, she is gone. I feel as if I've spent a suitable time grieving for her. It would be very wrong for me to give up women altogether, wouldn't it? And I feel you came into my life to inspire me to try again, to open my heart, my sweet muse."

He walked toward me with a seductive look in his eyes.

My knees went a little weak. Ghost or not, this was a very attractive man who clearly wanted me.

But when he stretched out his hands and touched my cheek with his icy fingers, I recoiled and came back to my senses.

I had mentioned Esme hoping to get him to remember his last days, so that he'd understand that he was dead.

That hadn't worked. I had to think of something else.

My reaction had clearly upset Euan. He wasn't used to women rejecting his advances. "What's wrong? Don't you like my touch?"

I decided to treat this situation the same as I would a Band-Aid.

Rip it off.

"That's the thing. You can't touch me, Euan. Haven't you noticed? You can't really touch anything material. It's because you aren't alive. You're dead. Have been for a long time."

Euan stared at me.

I held my breath.

I didn't know what his reaction might be.

Would he argue with me? He might even be angry and direct his wrath at me.

What I didn't expect was laughter.

Euan roared with amusement.

"Oh, I like that! You want to play little games with me? I love games. What do you want me to be? An undead creature? A vampire? Do you want me to…bite you?"

He inched closer, his hands raised as claws in a mock attempt to grab me.

I backed off until my back hit the windowsill. I half turned, and my gaze fell on the moonlit scene below.

I had an idea.

CHAPTER SIXTEEN

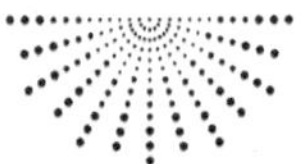

"Yes!" I exclaimed, ducking away so he couldn't reach me. I went to the door, then turned around.

"But I don't want to play here. There's a much more suitable place for our little game." I wiggled my eyebrows. "Follow me."

Euan chuckled. "I'd follow you anywhere, my sweet muse."

I ran down the spiral staircase, getting the flashlight out of my bag, and rushed across the foyer without looking at the spooky animals.

"Wait for me," Euan said.

I wanted him to follow me, but I didn't want him to catch up with me before we got to the destination I had in mind.

So I hurried down the stairs, crossed the hall, and pushed the door open to get outside. I spun around to get my bearings, and Euan was suddenly by my side.

"Where do you want to go?"

"Just follow me." I made my way to the back of the

castle, which wasn't that easy because the garden was hopelessly overgrown. There might have been a path before, but it wasn't visible anymore.

Out of breath, I finally made it to the little graveyard.

I turned around to face Euan. "Ta-da!"

He frowned, clearly unsure if he was on board with this. "You want to make love in a graveyard? That's an odd predilection. But…" He shrugged, then grinned. "Why not?"

I moved away from him again, weaving around overgrown and collapsed gravestones. "Wait…it has to be just right."

"What am I then? A ghoul? A vampire? A ghost?" Euan said with a mock-shuddering voice as he followed me.

I desperately tried to make out the inscriptions on the gravestones. It wasn't easy. The moonlight was bright enough, but the stones were old, and nobody had taken care of the graveyard for a long while.

But then I found it.

"A ghost!" I exclaimed in relief and pointed at the gravestone.

"What?" Euan came closer.

"Yes, read the inscription."

He did, and his demeanor changed from confusion to anger.

"Is this a joke?"

"No," I breathed. "What do you see?"

"It looks as if this is my gravestone. There's no other Sir Euan Campbell, and it has my date of birth on it. The year of death is this year. What's the meaning of this, Bethany?" His tone was now rather threatening.

I swallowed.

"It's almost a hundred years later, Euan. Haven't you

wondered about the way I dress and talk? It's not just because I'm American, but because I'm from the present. You have been dead all this time. You're a ghost."

Euan vigorously shook his head.

"No, no, no. This simply can't be true. I can't be buried here." He made a motion as if to grab and shake the headstone, but of course, he didn't succeed. His hands passed through the stone.

"See!" I called out in desperation. "You can't touch it. You can't touch anything. You couldn't touch me or the bureau drawer. Because you're a ghost."

Euan stopped as if frozen in shock, staring at his hands. He seemed to grasp for the first time that I was speaking the truth.

There was a dangerous spark in his eyes when he backed away, only to then to charge at the gravestone.

There was no resistance, so he ran right through it.

His face contorted into a mask of anger, and he roared, pointing at the stone as if it was to blame for the whole situation.

The stone shook, and the earth moved.

Scared, I ran to hide behind a big angel statue.

Laughing like a madman, Euan directed more of this ghostly power at the grave in front of him.

He might not be able to touch things, but he clearly had some dangerous poltergeist-like energy, and his frustration was channeled into a crazy delight in wielding such power.

"Stop," I cried. "Stop this." I obviously hadn't known what to expect when I used my "gift" to make a ghost realize he was dead, but getting into such a dangerous situation hadn't even been on my mental list of things that could happen. I was so far out of my depth, it wasn't even funny.

Either Euan didn't hear me, or he didn't care.

He carried on until the headstone was on the ground and the earth was all broken up, as if he was wielding an invisible tool to dig up the grave.

I was already scared out of my wits, but now I became completely petrified when the coffin—really just rotten wooden slabs that were barely holding together—rose out of the grave as if by magic, hovered there for a few moments, and then came crashing down to the ground.

Suddenly, everything became very still.

It was as if the energy went out of Euan. He sank to the ground, kneeling next to the remains of his coffin.

Hesitantly, I moved around the angel statue and approached him.

"Euan? Are you okay?"

My whole body tensed, ready to seek cover again if it looked as if rage would possess him once more.

But he just kneeled there, deflated, staring into the air.

I crept closer.

It had been almost a hundred years, so I was pretty certain there wouldn't be much left of his remains. I certainly didn't want to see that!

Still, a morbid sense of curiosity made me glance at the coffin.

There was something sparkly…metal, with the moonlight bouncing off it.

I realized this was what Euan was staring at.

Trying to ignore everything else that was in the coffin, I bent over and carefully picked up the metal item.

"What's this?" I whispered.

"My kilt pin with the Campbell clan crest above the Highland thistle," he said tonelessly.

He pointed at the same—but newer and shinier in its ghostly existence—pin on his kilt. "My mother had it made for me."

"You were buried with it." I said gently.

"So it's true. I don't exist anymore. I'm a ghost. How could I not have known all this time?" He looked at me helplessly.

I could only shrug. "I don't know. I don't know how this works."

"But...," he said, as if he only realized it now, "how come you can see me? You have a special ability to help me, don't you?"

"Apparently so. But I only learned about it a few days ago. I had no idea before I came to Scotland. You are the first ghost I've ever dealt with. I have no idea how this works. I thought, once you realized you were a ghost, that'd be enough. You don't by any chance see a bright light, do you?"

Euan looked around. Then he gave a sad smile and shook his head.

We sat there on the dirty ground in silence for a while.

"Maybe this has to do with my death," Euan offered. "How did I die?"

I looked at him in surprise. "You don't remember?"

"No."

"By all appearances, you died peacefully in your sleep of a heart attack. But, well, all things considered, it stands to reason that you were..."

I bit my lip because I didn't really want to say it.

Euan had no such qualms.

"Murdered?"

"Try to think about the last night you remember. Wasn't it the same night Esme disappeared? Maybe she had something to do with it."

"No... Not my Esme. No, she wouldn't..." He stared at what remained of the coffin, and his eyes widened. "Something is coming back to me."

He shuddered and went even paler than before. His

hand moved to his mouth, and he shook his head in horror. "Oh god."

"What? Do you recall it now? Was it Esme?"

"N…no, I don't know. But I do remember coming to in this coffin."

I stared at Euan in disbelief. "Coming to in the coffin? What do you mean?"

"I remember waking up in a dark, enclosed space. It took me a while to understand that I was buried alive. I screamed, I scratched my fingers bloody to claw myself out… To no avail."

"Oh my god." I had no clue what made a person turn into a ghost after death, but if a traumatic experience was the usual cause, being buried alive would do it.

"You must have only appeared dead, and then…" I swallowed. "Maybe you were poisoned, so that death was mimicked. I think I've read about something like that before."

Euan looked at me in disbelief. "But who in the world would do that to me? And why?"

I had a pretty good idea, but Euan didn't want to believe it, so I just shrugged.

We stayed silent for a minute or so, then I said, "I'll try to find out. Maybe knowing who was responsible will cause you to…" I made a helpless gesture "…move on."

"Whatever that means," Euan said tonelessly.

I struggled to get up. My limbs felt stiff. I tried to brush dirt off my top, but it was pointless. The jeans I might be able to wash, but the top was probably ruined.

It was the least of my worries.

"I'd better go now. But I'll try to find out what I can. I'll be back."

He said nothing.

I felt pretty useless as I walked away, casting glances over my shoulder at Euan every couple of steps until I'd rounded the castle and couldn't see the graveyard anymore.

Then I ran as fast as I could, as if a monster were chasing me, all the way to the cottage.

In my room, I stripped off my clothes and didn't even bother to go to the bathroom.

I just hid under the covers like a frightened child.

CHAPTER SEVENTEEN

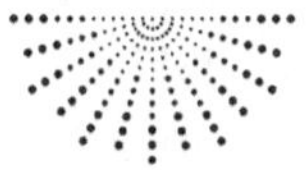

"Beth? Bethany?"

A voice with a Scottish accent called me.

"No, Euan," I murmured. "I don't know. I don't know how to help you."

"Bethany, wake up!" The voice was pretty insistent and pierced my consciousness.

I blinked and realized I'd been asleep.

"Beth!"

The voice didn't belong to Euan, but to Alex.

He was standing over me, a concerned look in his eyes.

"W…What? What's going on?"

I glanced around. I was in my room, in my bed. With a jolt, I remembered I'd crawled under the covers in my underwear earlier, so I pulled the sheet up to my neck.

"It's almost noon, and you've been fast asleep. I couldn't get you to wake up, so I was getting a little worried."

"Oh." I brushed my hair out of my face. "I'm so sorry. I couldn't get to sleep last night, and—"

"What's that?" He bent over and pulled something out

of my hair. It was grass. Probably from running through the overgrown garden.

"And…is that a streak of dirt in your face?"

"Umm… I went for a walk last night. Like I said, I couldn't go to sleep, so I thought fresh air might do the trick."

Alex gave me an amused look. "You went for a walk in the dark, through the woods?"

"Yes. And it worked, since I crashed as soon as I got back. Apparently I needed the sleep. Maybe delayed jet lag?"

Alex looked skeptical. "Maybe."

"Anyway, I'm sorry. That's not very professional of me. Did you want to…um…have me help with your work?"

I needed to remember that was also what I was here for. I was supposed to be Alex's muse, and Mrs. MacDonald had wanted us to give our working relationship a second chance.

"Um…sure, I mean… Aunt Mary said we should go out. Why don't we try tonight? We could go to Oban for dinner and a drink?"

"Let's do that." I forced a smile. "Now, if you don't mind…" I pointed with my chin toward the door. "I'd better get up."

"Oh. Sure. I made sandwiches for lunch. I already had some, but there are leftovers in the fridge. Please help yourself. I'll make a reservation for tonight, and then I'll go back to work."

"Thank you!"

He left, and I threw the covers back to climb out of bed.

I had a shower and washed my hair to get the grime off.

For once, I didn't put on any make-up. I just didn't have the energy, and I didn't care about Alex seeing me like that anymore. Then I dressed in the most casual outfit I'd packed—yoga pants and a T-shirt—and went to the kitchen.

The roast beef and horseradish sandwiches were delicious, but I would have eaten anything since I was as hungry as a hippo.

After lunch, I looked up the number for the Thistle Inn and called Mrs. MacDonald.

Luckily she was home, and she picked up on the first ring.

"Hi Bethany," she said, as if she was expecting my call. Maybe she had my number saved on her phone.

"I tried to help the ghost of Invercreran Castle, and I failed miserably," I blurted.

Mrs. MacDonald didn't seem perturbed by this at all. "Walk me through what happened," she said calmly.

I hesitated, a little scared of my own temerity. Mrs. MacDonald was Euan's daughter, and her mother might have killed her father. Did she really want to know?

Maybe I should have called one of the younger witches instead.

I stuck to the facts of what had happened the night before, not telling her anything about my suspicions about her mother.

"So what I did hasn't worked," I summed up my frustrations. "But I also don't really know what I'm supposed to do here."

I wanted Mrs. MacDonald to tell me how my gift worked. But she didn't seem to know either.

"These sorts of abilities never come with explicit instructions," she said, as if she was reading my mind. "Usually older and experienced female relatives provide guidance for younger witches. Sadly, in your case—"

"I can't talk to my mother about this," I interrupted. "She told me she just ignored any ghosts who ever spoke to her and they went away, and that I should do the same. She thinks it's a sign of mental illness. At the very least, she's going to be worried about me, and I don't want to do that to her. She might even have me hospitalized. I can't really blame her for being traumatized about this, after what happened to her mother…but it would be such a relief to talk to someone with the same ability."

"You *are* going to have to discuss it with your mother eventually," Mrs. MacDonald said in a sensible tone. "It won't do to hide such a big part of yourself from her. Probably not over the phone, though," she conceded when I started to protest. "But there's one other person who might be more open to this conversation. Kirsty."

"My grandmother? I don't even know where she is, since my mother hasn't been in contact with her for ages. Also, she's in an institution, right? Is she even…I don't know, lucid enough to have that kind of talk?"

Mrs. MacDonald was silent for a moment.

"Your grandmother hasn't been confined to a mental health facility for many years, Bethany. She's perfectly fine. She now lives in a retirement community in Florida."

I was shocked speechless.

The image of my grandmother I'd had in my mind all this time—admittedly, a very cliched image derived from old movies, where spaced-out patients in white floaty nightgowns and wild hair wandered the mental hospital corridors or sat in rocking chairs—didn't match up with a Florida retiree.

"I promised I wouldn't say anything before you were fully ready, but I think you are. Kirsty and I have been exchanging letters for years. We cooked this whole thing up together. Since her daughter doesn't want to have anything to do with her, Kirsty feared you wouldn't want to have contact either. She has spent many years coming to terms with her ability after she suffered so much as a young woman. She still wants to pass down her legacy to you."

I didn't know what to say, so I stammered something in an effort to express my indignation. It was bad enough that Mrs. MacDonald had gotten me here under false pretenses, but my own grandmother… I felt like I was being controlled and that everyone, including my mother, had kept me purposefully in the dark.

"Does Mom know about this?" I finally articulated a clear question.

"About you coming here to discover your gift? No, she—"

"No, I mean, does she know about Grandma living in Florida and being…well, I guess?"

"I think Kirsty has tried to reach out every so often, so she probably does."

I got that everything to do with her mother had been so painful for my mom that she only wanted to safeguard herself against getting hurt again. And I understood she just wanted to protect me too.

But she hadn't done me a favor in keeping this from me. It was something I needed to deal with, no matter how difficult, and by wrapping me in cotton wool, Mom had sort of stunted my development, not just as a witch, but as a human being.

Alex had basically called me naive, spoiled, and shallow upon my arrival here, and I had been outraged. The truth was, he hadn't been so far off the mark.

But I couldn't even blame my mother, who had only ever done her best and cocooned me out of love, so I wouldn't have to go through whatever she had gone through. Ultimately, this had also been her survival strategy.

How much damage would confronting her with this do?

Would she completely break apart?

Or could this lead to true healing for three generations of women with the same special gift?

There was a lot I had to think about.

"I don't know what to do about my mom and Kirsty," I said to Mrs. MacDonald. "I don't know if I can just call my grandmother up… It's…a lot. I'll call you back."

I had to clear my head, so I went for a walk.

When I let Alex know I was leaving, he said. "Again? You seem to love your walks."

I just shrugged, distracted by my own thoughts.

My feet automatically took me along the winding track to the castle.

I hesitated in front of the gate, but then I went in. I'd forgotten to lock it last night—and then I remembered that the entrance door would be open too.

Even though I didn't know what to do about my own family, I could still try to help Euan. It would lend me a bit of confidence to do something good with my gift, and maybe that would even enable me to speak to my mom and grandma.

Last night had been very emotional. It was entirely possible that Euan now had a better idea of how I could help him. Perhaps he'd recalled more about his last hours as a living person?

I stepped into the big hall. I hadn't brought a flashlight, but my phone was in my pocket, so I took it out and turned on the flashlight app.

Nothing had changed in here. The sheets were off the Chesterfield suite just as I'd left them last night.

"Euan?" I called, my voice echoing eerily in the cavernous room.

I only heard a faint bark again.

Shivering, I moved up the grand staircase.

This time, there wasn't the same pull from the tower room. Maybe because I'd already answered that call.

I went there anyway, since it was Euan's chamber and I hoped to find him there.

When I opened the oak door, I got a bit of shock, however.

It wasn't just the terrible smell—certainly nothing like the scent of roses this time.

The room didn't look at all like it had in my vision or last night, when I'd had the encounter with Euan.

The furniture was in the same place—the four-poster bed, the bureau, the card table. But everything looked as if it hadn't been touched in a hundred years, like the rest of the castle. It was covered in dust, and the fabrics hadn't stood the test of time.

The jacquard canopy was in tatters, and the bedspread looked as if it had been eaten by mice and other critters.

Unlike downstairs, the drapes were pretty much coming down too. Enough light filtered through the dirty window that the decay was even more visible.

Bureau and bed might be able to be restored to their magnificent splendor, and ordinarily my mind would have gone there.

There was something else commanding my attention, though.

The card table was set for a romantic dinner, just as it had been the night before. The silver of the cloches was tarnished, and there was no bubbling liquid in the crystal flutes, but still…

It seemed incongruent for everything to have been left in this room.

Yes, after Euan's death the castle hadn't been inhabited, but in reality it hadn't been like the Sleeping Beauty fairy tale I had imagined. It wasn't like everything had stopped with Euan's last breath and the castle just "went to sleep" in this snapshot of events in the past.

Euan had been buried, and someone had taken care of the castle. Before leaving, they had covered the furniture with sheets. They wouldn't have just left food dishes in this room.

I also had an inkling that the foul smell that had assaulted my nostrils upon entering was originating from this table.

The closer I moved toward it, the worse it got. And did I detect a buzzing sound?

I had a bad feeling about this, but I had to check. I pinched my nose with one hand and then stretched out the other from as far away as possible to lift one cloche.

A cloud of flies dispersed, and I dropped the cloche. It clattered to the floor.

My hand went to my mouth to stop myself from gagging.

There were the remains of what I assumed was half a chicken, bones and all, on the plate. There might have been other food items, but it was hard to tell with all the maggots wriggling and the flies buzzing.

I turned away, ready to bolt out of there, and almost bumped into someone.

In fact, I did bump into the person, passing halfway through their incorporeal presence.

As soon as my body registered the cold, I withdrew. "Sorry," I mumbled, looking up at Euan's face.

At least I expected it to be Euan's face.

He was the only ghost I'd met here—actually, the only specter I'd consciously met, ever. So who else would I expect in this castle?

I'd thought he was the only ghost here.

I was wrong.

CHAPTER EIGHTEEN

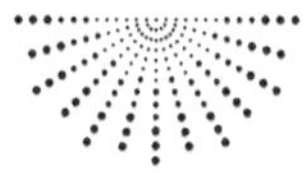

"My apologies, Madam," the middle-aged woman in an old-fashioned dress said, and she whizzed past me.

She picked up the cloche and put it back, mercifully covering the decaying food and maggots.

"Should have cleared this away earlier," the woman muttered to herself. "There's no excuse for it, really. No excuse. But everyone's gone, and I'm the only one to look after Sir Euan and the castle, and it's a big place. I'm not complaining, mind," she prattled on, as she took the tray with the plates and glasses and carried it out of the room. "I'm very lucky to have my position here, I know that. And Sir Euan would be lost without me. He always says it. What would I do without you, Hattie, he says…"

Wide-eyed, I followed Hattie down the spiral staircase and through the room with the animals.

I was fascinated that she could carry the tray. Either ghosts could touch things from the real world after all, and this housekeeper ghost was doing just that, so to anyone else it would look as if the tray were floating in the air. Or the tray wasn't real and was instead part of a ghostly reality I was privy to, thanks to my abilities. That was entirely possible, because last night I had seen the room the way Euan, the ghost, had perceived it, namely the way it had been in his lifetime.

That begged the question as to why the housekeeper had "conjured up" food items that were at least a month old.

Maybe the food was real after all, something from my time that the housekeeper could make part of her ghostly existence. Just like with Sir Euan's room—as a Lothario, clearly his domain in the castle. The material scaffolding was there, since it still existed in the current time. So he could make it "his" on his ghostly plane of existence.

I stopped myself from trying to figure out the logic behind what I was seeing since it was probably pointless anyway to try to make rhyme or reason out of it.

Instead, I tried to focus on the fact that I was seeing another ghost.

I followed Hattie all the way to a subbasement level, where I suspected the kitchen was, and interestingly, she didn't seem to mind. The housekeeper rarely paused her nonstop chatter, telling me—or, more accurately, herself—about the chores she still needed to complete that day. She also worried out loud about Sir Euan. Was he eating enough? Was he entertaining too much? Then Hattie talked with some annoyance about someone called Archie. I was wondering who that could be when I heard the faint barking again.

Suddenly, a huge dog bounded along the hallway, coming toward us.

I wasn't exaggerating; it really was humongous. Its back came up to my waist, and when it jumped up on me, its paws on my shoulders, its head right in front of mine, it could have easily knocked me down. I'm a dog person, but I have to admit I screamed.

"Archie, down!" Hattie exclaimed, more annoyed than alarmed.

But the dog was a ghost, and all that happened was that I got really cold when his paws and legs passed through my body.

"Don't worry, Madam," Hattie said. "Archie still thinks of himself as a wee puppy. He doesn't know his own strength. He's as sweet a dog as can be, really."

"Okay…" I said skeptically, still a little out of breath.

"Sir Euan got him as a guard dog, but it soon turned out that Archie wouldn't be good at frightening anyone. He just wants to play."

The dog now looked at me expectantly, wagging his tail with excitement. He had a gray, shaggy coat, a long face with a short muzzle, and long hair falling into his dark, soulful eyes. I assumed Archie was an Irish wolfhound, although I'd never seen one in real life.

Now that I'd gotten over my initial scare, I was sad I couldn't pet him. Archie clearly wanted me to. "You probably haven't gotten a good scratch in all this time, huh, buddy?"

If he'd been Sir Euan's dog, Archie must have passed away around the time of his master's death, which meant he'd been roaming the castle as a doggy ghost for a long while.

The thought made me wonder how many ghosts haunted Invercreran. Would I have to help each and every one move on?

I felt an acute sense of being overwhelmed. I had no idea how to do any of this.

Hattie had already carried on walking along the hallway, and I hurried to catch up with her before she rounded the corner.

I didn't want her to disappear. Hattie was from Sir Euan's time—as was Archie. Maybe they were only here because they were Euan's faithful servant and companion, and they'd move on if their master did.

I hoped Hattie could help me. She'd lived in the castle with Sir Euan and might have useful information.

We arrived in the kitchen, Archie right behind us. Hattie scolded him, but in a good-natured tone that told me she didn't really mind. The housekeeper probably made the exception often, because the dog lay down on a rug in the corner as if it was his usual spot.

The kitchen was clearly Hattie's domain, just like Sir Euan's chamber had been his. I had the suspicion that if I'd seen this room without the ghost in it, it would have looked very different. Now I perceived it as a spick-and-span, fully operating kitchen from the beginning of the twentieth century. The massive cast-iron cooking range must have been used for a century before that even, because it made the stove in Alex's cottage look state-of-the-art.

There was a freshly plucked pheasant on the table, and I really, really hoped there wasn't some kind of maggot-infested equivalent in reality.

In any case, when Hattie offered me refreshments, I thought it safer to decline.

I was really curious to know who Hattie thought I was.

She wouldn't have let me follow her into the kitchen if she'd thought I was a guest of Sir Euan's. She would have treated me with more deference, and she surely wouldn't have told me all the little things concerning the castle household.

But if she'd thought I was a servant, she'd have put me to work already and not offered me food and drink.

Maybe I was overthinking things.

Hattie was a ghost, and she might not be terribly aware, having been caught in some kind of daily-chores loop for almost a hundred years.

I decided to just ask her what I wanted to know.

I'd soon find out if she found it weird that a random woman in twenty-first-century garb stood in her kitchen interrogating her.

What was the worst that could happen?

After all, Hattie couldn't do anything to me.

I pushed away any thought of the havoc Euan's anger had caused the previous night.

"So, Hattie..." I began. "How come you're doing everything by yourself? Where's the rest of the staff?"

"Everyone's gone," Hattie said, shaking her head while deftly peeling a potato. "I don't blame them, really. But I couldn't let Sir Euan fend for himself. I've looked after him ever since he was a wee bairn. He has his faults, to be sure. Still, I couldn't leave him."

She put the potato down to gather the peel, and when she moved her hand, the peel was gone, but the potato was in its original state again. She proceeded to peel it once more.

I blinked in astonishment. Well, it was no surprise she couldn't manage to catch up with her chores if they were indeed never ending.

"Where else would I go, anyway?" Hattie continued. "This has been my home for so many years, I couldn't imagine anything else. I haven't even gone home to Arrochar for, oh, I don't know how many years, so—"

My ears perked up. "Arrochar?" Hattie came from the village next to the one my ancestors had come from—and Esme too. It couldn't be a coincidence.

"You didn't by any chance know Esme MacDonald from home? Did you help her get employment here?"

"No, I didn't know her before. The last time I was home, Esme hadn't even been born. But my cousin worked here for a while, and when we had an opening for a new maid—they never seem to want to stick it out, these young lasses—she mentioned the wee MacDonald lass was looking."

I could very well imagine why maids didn't last long at the castle. Sir Euan must have made it a habit to "entertain" the young and pretty girls, only to drop them like hot potatoes at his convenience.

Hattie continued speaking. "I'd known her mother, though, and her grandmother. Everyone knew *them*."

"Were they…special in some way?" I treaded carefully.

But the chatty housekeeper had no intention of holding out on me anyway. "You could say that. There was a group of women who knew about healing and soothsaying and charms and all that. Esme's family was involved with them. Esme too. One of them came to visit a few times, a beautiful blond lass. Esme showed her the garden."

"So why do you think Esme ran away? Is it true that she was with child and Sir Euan wouldn't do the honorable thing?"

Hattie dropped the potato. Her mild expression changed, and her eyes glittered dangerously. "Sir Euan wouldn't do anything like that. Don't you go starting rumors about him." She held up the knife she'd used to peel the potato and came toward me.

I didn't know if she was actually threatening me or if the knife was even real, but I didn't want to risk it.

I backed away, holding up my hands. "Of course not. Maybe there was a misunderstanding. Esme might have misinterpreted the situation."

The fire went out of Hattie's eyes as fast as it had ignited. She went back to the table to resume peeling her potato.

"Could be."

"Or maybe she was just really shocked when Euan passed away like that, and she ran off."

I observed Hattie's reaction carefully, but she didn't

seem the least bit anxious about me mentioning the fact that Sir Euan was dead.

Instead, she acknowledged it. "We were all very upset when that happened."

Huh. So did Hattie know she was dead and that Euan was a spirit too?

Yet again, ghost logic had me mystified.

"Could I see Esme's room?"

"Sure." Hattie wiped her hands on a dish towel and went up a small set of stairs behind the kitchen. "I'm not sure what you hope to find. She took everything she owned with her."

"Of course," I said, a little disappointed. Still, seeing her room was my best shot at learning more about Esme.

Hattie was clearly blind to Esme's motives, so she couldn't see a reason why Esme might have killed Sir Euan. It was pointless discussing it further with the ghostly housekeeper.

But Hattie could still be a source of information. She'd already given me the idea that Esme had been in cahoots with the Tarbet coven.

The pretty blond lass interested in the garden could have been anyone, of course, but the description really reminded me of Penny. It could have been one of her ancestors who had visited Esme here.

It all fit together in my mind, because I had the strong suspicion that Euan had been poisoned by Esme. Surely there were plants that could be used to poison someone in such a way that the victim seemed dead and then regained consciousness days later, and someone with Penny's gift might have provided Esme with the necessary know-how.

Esme's room in the servant's quarters was tiny, with whitewashed walls and dark wooden ceiling beams. There was just a narrow cot and a plain dresser.

"See," Hattie said, opening the top drawer. "Esme left nothing behind."

I went through the drawers myself.

Hattie was right. They were completely empty.

I thought about the hidden compartment in Euan's bureau, but this plain wooden chest of drawers probably wouldn't have anything like that. Still, I was pretty desperate, so I took my time feeling around inside the drawer.

"Well, I can't stand around idly. I have too much to do," Hattie said, then disappeared.

"Wai…" I wanted to rush after her because I didn't know when I'd have an opportunity to talk to her again.

Just then, my fingers touched something other than rough wood. It was stuck to the bottom of the drawer above, possibly caught by a splinter, and I suspected it was a piece of paper. I carefully extracted it.

I jumped for joy when I saw what it was.

It looked like a page ripped out of a high-end notebook. The paper was thick and had a handcrafted quality to it, and it was brownish with age.

It surprised me to see that Esme had owned what appeared to be expensive paper, but Euan had mentioned she'd liked to sketch, so maybe someone had gifted it to her.

There was a drawing on the paper, and I thought it was very good.

It was a botanical illustration of a plant with green leaves, purple bell-shaped flowers, and black round berries.

I stared at it for a moment, not quite able to believe my luck.

Then I got my phone out of my jeans pocket and dialed a number.

"Penny, I need to ask you something."

CHAPTER NINETEEN

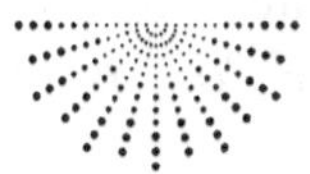

Alex and I were sitting in a charming pub in Oban's harbor, a magnificent view of Oban Bay visible from our table by the window.

I was staring out but, admittedly, without really seeing what was outside.

"Is everything okay?" Alex asked hesitantly. "Is this too…rustic for you? Oban really doesn't have many modern cocktail bars or clubs, so—"

"Oh no! This is lovely. I'm just distracted, that's all."

"I noticed." Alex furrowed his brows. "Should we maybe do this another time? My aunt really pushed us together, and I understand if you're having second thoughts."

I sighed and took a sip of the delicious regional cider Alex had gotten me from the bar.

"And you had very different expectations of what this job was going to entail," Alex carried on.

I laughed. "Yes, you could say that."

Alex spread out his palms. Knowing what works of art his hands were capable of creating, I couldn't help but find them very sexy.

"Look, I'd totally understand if you want to call it quits, if this is not at all like you imagined. You have every right to do that, you know."

"Would you like me to leave?"

I didn't say this in an accusatory tone; I was merely curious. He'd been so dismissive of me when I'd first arrived. Considering the way I'd behaved, I didn't even blame him that much. He'd had his prejudices, and I'd had my preconceptions.

But we'd gotten to know each other a little better over the last couple of days, and I'd had the feeling our relationship was changing. Maybe I was wrong and it was only because *I* had been changing.

I wasn't going to do a three-sixty, though. I was still Bethany Prince, and if he didn't like me by now, a great muse-artist relationship probably wasn't on the horizon. I didn't want him to keep me on as his muse only because his aunt said so and because he was financially dependent on her.

"No," he said, to my relief. "I actually like your company. You're very different from the women I know, and I admit that I probably judged you too quickly." He grimaced. "I'm truly sorry about that. My aunt might be right about…I don't know, a certain amount of friction needed to stir something up in me…"

When I grinned, he blushed. "I mean, professionally speaking. To stir inspiration and creativity."

"Sure."

"But we don't need to force anything here, no matter what my aunt wants. She seems so sure you're the right person for the job, but ultimately it's something we need to decide for ourselves."

I put the empty glass of down. Alex was right. We had to make a decision about our professional relationship soon. But it wasn't fair for him not to know all the details.

Besides, I wanted him to see me for what I really was. How could he do that if he didn't know about the massive new part of my identity I'd just discovered?

I got why the witches of the Tarbet coven kept their community and their gifts a secret. Although even they confided in outsiders from time to time. But with my family history, I just felt like I needed to come out of the psychic closet, so to speak.

"I have to admit something here. Your aunt had an ulterior motive when she chose me as your muse."

Alex furrowed his brows. "Oh, really?"

"Yes. There was another job she had in mind for me."

"What would that be?"

He looked at me intently with his moss-green eyes, so much like Euan Campbell's that I got flustered.

"Umm, well…it's got to do with the castle. The furniture, to be exact. Some of the furniture and other antiques could be very valuable. I did special training during my studies, so this is sort of my expertise. Your aunt wants me to appraise, restore, and sell the antiques. The proceeds could then be invested in the castle's restoration." This wasn't really what I'd wanted to say to Alex, but it was true. I'd talked to Mrs. MacDonald on the phone earlier, proposing the plan, and she'd agreed.

Alex's eyes widened. "Really? Don't get me wrong, but I'm surprised she would have chosen you for this job, bringing you all the way over from the States. And you only just graduated, so you don't have any experience. It seems to me she would have been better off hiring a local antique dealer."

"I'm not offended. Of course you're right. I'll be working with someone local who has more experience."

"Then I really don't get why she flew you out here—"

"There's something else," I blurted out. "I have

another, more unique skill…um, a skill needed before the castle can be renovated."

I would have liked to take a sip of my drink, but my glass was empty. My mouth was parched, and I felt like my throat was closing up.

I tried my best to speak anyway. "When I got here, you told me that nobody stays at the castle. There's a reason nobody likes to go in there, and when you followed me there that night, you also felt it, didn't you? We talked about it. A sort of…energy. A haunting energy."

Alex stared at me for a moment, even though I hardly dared meet his eyes. Then he said. "Are you talking about the ghost?"

"Yes," I exhaled. "Your aunt wants me to get rid of the ghost of Euan Campbell. See, one of my ancestors is originally from Tarbet, and she left because of her special gift. The ability to communicate with spirits. She was running away from it, actually. Your aunt knew this, kept tabs on her and her offspring. I had no idea about any of it. Well, my grandmother Kirsty has the gift, but she was declared mentally ill when my mother was a child…" I talked faster and faster, spilling out the entire story.

When I was done, I stared down at the wooden table, perfectly still, waiting for what would happen next.

Would Alex storm out?

Call me crazy?

Maybe even call someone to pick me up or have me committed?

When he didn't say anything for what seemed like an eternity, I whispered, "You can call your aunt, and she'll confirm what I said."

Alex took my hand. Surprised, I looked up. "I don't need to call her, Bethany. I believe you. I was just really shocked at what you and your family have been through."

"You…believe me?" I searched his gaze for a hint of mockery, but he seemed perfectly serious.

Alex nodded. "I know about my aunt."

"But she said you—"

"She thinks I don't know anything. Takes me for a fool." He grinned, and I had to smile in return.

We looked into each other's eyes until someone next to us cleared his throat. "Excuse me. Careful, the plates are hot."

The server set down the food we'd ordered earlier, and we both leaned back in our seats so there was space on the table for the steaming plates spilling over with fish and chips and mushy peas.

"Condiments are on the table there." He pointed. "Enjoy."

"Thanks," Alex and I said in unison.

We the server was gone, Alex asked if I wanted anything. I agreed to try salt and vinegar on my fish and chips.

"Anything else to drink?"

"I'd love another cider."

Once he got back, we tucked into our food, which was delicious—even with the salt and vinegar, although I secretly vowed to stick with ketchup next time.

We talked some more. Alex told me about his suspicions where his aunt was concerned. He wasn't too far off the mark thinking her to be a witch with clairvoyant abilities—although, of course, what I knew about Mrs. MacDonald barely scratched the surface.

I tried my best to stay vague in my answers and neither confirm nor deny anything he said. Alex didn't know about the coven, and I felt I didn't have the right to let him in on the secret of the "women's club."

Then I told him more about Euan Campbell, even

though I didn't go into detail about what had happened on our "date" the other night.

Alex was a bit shocked that I had gone there at night, after what had happened during my previous visit. "Weren't you scared? I mean, could he do something to you?"

"He can't hurt me," I said, even though that wasn't strictly true. But I'd downplayed Euan's fit of rage in my retelling for Alex. "Sure, going into a haunted castle at night, meeting up with a ghost, is a bit anxiety inducing. I'm not going to lie."

"Maybe it's something you'll get used to as you encounter more ghosts."

"Perhaps." I told him about seeing the ghosts of the housekeeper and Archie, the dog, today.

"How many bloody ghosts inhabit the castle?" Alex exclaimed. "Do you have to get rid of them all?"

I shrugged. "I don't know. Maybe the housekeeper and the dog will go when Euan moves on. It seems as if they've stayed out of loyalty to him. It could be that ghosts who stay on earth voluntarily don't have such a…I don't know, strong haunting energy, that they bother the living."

Alex frowned in confusion. "I thought Euan had moved on already. You didn't meet him at the castle today, did you? Just the housekeeper? Maybe discovering his grave did the trick."

"Hmm. It's a possibility. I hope so. But I think I have to determine what happened to him. Figure out how he died."

I hadn't gone into the poisoning theory, had only said that I didn't believe he'd died peacefully of natural causes. It was still a delicate issue, with Esme being Mary MacDonald's mother. I didn't want to blame her for something until I had proof.

"How would you be able to do that, after all these years? I mean, what do you suppose happened to him?"

"What if he was murdered? Maybe I need to figure that out for him to move on. Get him justice by naming the murderer, you know?"

Alex raised an eyebrow. "Is that even possible, since so much time has passed? And also… Murder? That sounds a bit dangerous."

"It's not like the murderer could exact his revenge on me." I tried to make light of it. "You said yourself, it's such a long time ago. They would be dead themselves."

"Hmm."

"Well, let's wait and see. Maybe Euan has already moved on, after all."

The server cleared away our empty plates, and Alex went to the bar for more drinks.

I visited the bathroom, and on my way back, I passed the jukebox.

I put on "I Got a Feeling" from Black Eyed Peas and marched up to the table.

"May I have this dance?" I grinned.

Alex looked around in surprise. "Nobody is dancing."

"I know. That doesn't mean we can't, though."

"Oh…umm…"

"Come on. Didn't your aunt say you should open yourself up to new experiences? And that we should rub up against each other? Dancing quite literally means we're rubbing up against each other, so…" I wiggled my eyebrows, which made Alex laugh.

He took my hand and got up.

"Does that mean you want to stay on as my muse?"

I looked up at him, right into his green eyes. "Yes. I mean, I can't leave anyway. I have a castle full of ghosts and antique furniture that needs me. I could stay somewhere else, I guess. But it wouldn't be the same. I've gotten to like our little cottage. That is…if you'll have me…"

Alex put one hand on my waist and one on my shoulder. I was prepared to flinch, bracing myself for the icy feeling. But this wasn't a ghost who touched me, this was a warm-blooded man. It felt good. "Yes," he said. "Let's do this."

I laughed, and he spun me around.

I can honestly claim that I didn't think about ghosts anymore for the rest of that wonderful evening.

CHAPTER TWENTY

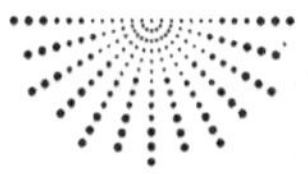

The next day, I took another train ride to Tarbet to visit Penny.

I brought the drawing with me, even though I'd already snapped a photo on my phone and forwarded it to Penny following our brief conversation yesterday.

The herb witch had immediately identified the plant as belladonna and named its poisonous qualities.

But she'd wanted to do more research for our meeting today.

After I arrived at Penny's cottage, she led me to her little garden shed.

Inside, she held up a plant, and I took a step back, since it looked exactly like the botanical illustration.

I'd read that belladonna was especially dangerous because it looked so pretty and inviting with its purple flowers and juicy, almost black berries. But to me, it looked dark and foreboding, probably because I knew about its deadly applications and suspected the role it had played in Sir Euan's death.

"Don't worry, the plant can't do anything to you if you look at it," Penny joked. "You can even touch it."

"No, thank you."

"Like all plants, belladonna, also known as deadly nightshade or devil's cherry, has its healing qualities too. Like the old adage says, the dose makes the poison."

"The names don't really inspire confidence," I said, but I moved closer to look at the plant.

"It usually blooms in late summer, and the berries appear even a little later, from August to October, so I helped this specimen along a little, just so you could see it in all its glory," Penny said.

"So do you use it?" I asked. "Do you grow this in your garden?"

"Yes, even though it has such a bad rep and it's the stereotypical witchy plant. Supposedly, witches use it as part of a flying ointment."

"Oh. Jem doesn't, does she?" I'd witnessed the weather witch fly high into the air the other night.

"No. She doesn't need to take anything. Anyway, belladonna has hallucinogenic qualities, so the witches might have just believed they were flying."

"Oh dear. I know little about drugs, so I don't quite understand. How can hallucinogenic qualities be used for medical purposes?"

"It's useful in psychotherapy. But the plant has other applications. Back in the day, women used to use belladonna eye drops to dilate the pupils and make themselves more attractive, and now it is regularly used to diagnose visual impairments. In addition, it has antispasmodic effects, so in low doses it can be used to treat epilepsy, asthma, colic, and even constipation. Aside from that, belladonna is actually really valuable to the ecosystem. Birds can eat the berries, and butterflies and bumblebees pollinate the flowers. It's a good plant to have in an herb witch's garden."

Penny put the plant down on the table and moved over to a cabinet.

She grabbed a stack of books—they looked like the old journal I'd found the other day.

"Are these grimoires?" I asked.

Penny nodded. "I looked up my ancestors' records of belladonna usage. Let's just say it was used a lot. So we can assume they had a good grasp of the dosages needed to treat someone with belladonna."

"It's possible, then, that one of your ancestors gave Esme the relevant information?"

"Yes, and I also know who it was." Penny triumphantly held up one journal. "My great-grandmother Gillian."

She opened the book, and I rushed to her side. "Did she write it down?" My voice squealed with excitement.

"Sort of." Penny showed me an entry, but it was just one row of letters and numbers, and I couldn't make heads or tails of it until Penny pointed out that the beginning said E MD, which she said had to mean Esme MacDonald.

"Are you sure?"

"Positive. The first letters in the row are always the name of the patient or customer. And the date matches up, see?" She pointed at the date on top of the page. It was only days before Euan had died.

"What does the rest mean?"

"I'm still figuring it out."

"Okay." I tried to suppress my disappointment. What Penny had found wasn't exactly hard evidence.

"Do you think it's possible to poison someone with belladonna so they look dead to a medical examiner, only for them to come out of that state in their grave?"

"Absolutely." Penny beamed. "Remember, I told you about the hallucinogens? They're also called tropane alkaloids. A high dose can be used to sedate someone, and an even higher dose can lead to a coma-like state. Breathing would become extremely shallow, and the heart rate would slow down so much that if someone just checked breathing and pulse they'd assume the person was dead. I mean, with our current medical technologies and forensic capabilities, it might not pass by doctors and medical examiners today if someone was in such a state due to, say, atropine poisoning. But back then? I'd say it's absolutely possible."

"Hmm. If they buried him quickly, and then he woke up in the coffin, realizing he'd been buried alive…"

"That's a horrible, traumatizing way to go, and it wouldn't be surprising if such a death would prevent a soul from finding eternal rest," Penny ended my sentence.

I gave a sad nod. "So do you think Esme got the dosage wrong, after all? Even though Gillian instructed her properly. She didn't give him quite enough belladonna to kill him?"

"Or she got it exactly right." Penny mused, leafing through Gillian's grimoire.

"Esme wanted to get revenge on Euan, so she made him die a most horrible death. That's unimaginably cruel, but if I'm right, Esme had a motive. Do you think your great-grandmother would have helped her, though? Or did Esme merely take advantage of her?"

"I'm only starting to crack the codes in Gillian's grimoire," Penny answered. "But it looks to me as if Gillian was dabbling in dark magic around the same time this happened. I think she turned over a new leaf shortly afterward." Penny showed me a page with a date on it.

"Hey, I can read this," I said, pointing at a word, careful not to touch the page. I didn't want to get an electric shock again. "Doesn't that say chamomile?

"It does. Gillian did much less with her herb magic after this date, and she clearly didn't feel the need to code as much, probably because everything was so harmless. Here. I MacL. Peppermint infusion. Digestion," Penny read out aloud. "You hardly need to be an herb witch to prescribe someone a mint tea for an upset tummy."

"If our theory is right and Esme really killed Euan this way, using information Gillian had given her, it might have shaken your great-grandmother up. She changed her ways and didn't use black magic anymore."

"It looks like it." Penny turned a few more pages. "Look, there are spells at the back of the journal. Gillian could have pretended they were poems, had the journal fallen into the wrong hands, but there's a code at the top, and I think it might correspond to codes in the entries featuring herbal ingredients."

We read some of the spells in silence. Suddenly, something caught my attention. "Hey, look at this."

Yarrow and hemlock to find peace,
Add foxglove for sweet release,
Reverse the dark, restore the light,
A final kiss will end this plight

"That sounds like a spell that might end a ghostly existence to me," I said.

Penny looked at me askance. "You deduced that from those words?"

"It's more of a feeling," I admitted, now doubting myself. "Forget it."

"No, there might be something to it. Yarrow, hemlock, and foxglove…" Penny put a finger to her lips, thinking. "They can be an antidote to belladonna."

"Do you think your great-grandmother might have come up with ways to reverse the dark magic she'd dabbled in before she turned herself around?" I asked excitedly.

"Hmm. Let's see if we can find the code in the entry she made on that date I showed you, the one I think refers to Esme."

I held my breath but let it out in a disappointed sigh when Penny turned the pages back and shook her head.

Penny closed the book. "I need to spend a little more time analyzing Gillian's grimoire."

Patience really wasn't one of my best qualities. "You know what? Let me try something that might make this process go a little faster."

I asked Penny to open to the page with the spell again.

Then I took a few cleansing breaths, closed my eyes, tried to focus on what I wanted to know, and put my palm on the writing on the page.

I don't know how much time passed, maybe a few seconds, maybe minutes.

When I removed my hand and opened my eyes again, Penny looked at me with an eager expression.

"And?" she said. "Did you see anything?"

I smiled and nodded.

"I know how we can help Euan move on. Do you by any chance have yarrow, hemlock, and foxglove on hand?"

CHAPTER TWENTY-ONE

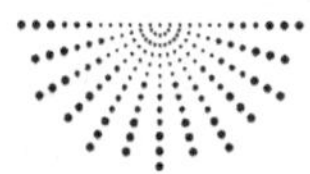

The next day, I drove up to the castle in Alex's beat-up old car. I had a stepladder, dusters, a mop, and an entire array of cleaning products with me.

One of my tasks today would be to take down the drapes and the sheets in the downstairs hall, clean, and hopefully discover antique treasures we could restore and sell.

I also hoped to run into a ghost or two so I could make some progress in helping those who haunted the castle move on.

Only a few days ago I would never have hoped for such an encounter, I realized with amusement. The idea of seeing and communicating with ghosts would have frightened me, and I had to admit that I still had some trepidation where the tower room was concerned.

It wasn't easy to forget how terrified I'd been my first night up there.

I felt pretty comfortable downstairs in the castle, though, especially after I'd taken down the thick dark drapes and light flooded through the tall windows.

I also discovered that I was thrilled to see my first ghost of the day, who announced himself with a bark.

The huge gray hound came bounding into the hall, clearly elated to find me there.

"Archie!" I called out, shivering as he jumped through me again. I tried to pet him, but my fingers just went through what I imagined being coarse hair. It felt like sticking a hand into the freezer instead of touching a warm dog. That made me a little sad—and Archie too, I thought.

At least we could play fetch, which we did with a sponge for a while. Amazingly, Archie could integrate the sponge into his ghostly plane of existence and pick his toy up and bring it to me.

That made me wonder if he could do that with my petting hands, if we tried hard enough and once we'd gotten to know each other better.

I had so much fun with the dog that I forgot my goal for a moment. If I did my job right, we wouldn't get to know each other better because I'd help Archie move on to a place where he belonged and where he was at peace.

But then Hattie came in and reminded me. "You're just getting him excited, Madam," she scolded me. "He makes such a mess when he runs around like that. Look at this." She shook her head, pointing at the heap of sheets I'd pulled off the furniture.

"I'm sorry," I said, definitely feeling chastised. "Is everything okay?" Hattie seemed in more of a tizzy than yesterday, but maybe it was just because of the disturbance in the downstairs hall.

"I have so much to do." The housekeeper wrung her hands. "I can't possibly make the trip to the store. But I'm out of chocolate *and* honey. Sir Euan always wants his spiced cocoa at night. He'll be very cross with me if he doesn't get his cocoa tonight."

"He has it every night before he goes to sleep?" I asked.

Penny and I had been wondering how Esme had disguised the taste of the atropine poison. Spiced hot chocolate with lots of honey would have done the trick.

"Yes!" Hattie exclaimed, looking crestfallen.

"You know what, don't worry about it, Hattie," I said. "I'll fetch chocolate and honey from the store today, and I'll bring Sir Euan his cocoa tonight."

"Oh, would you do that?"

"Of course. And I'll take care of the mess in here too."

"Wonderful. You're a big help. Thank you."

"No problem."

"Then I'll get back to peeling the potatoes." Hattie rushed off.

Knowing this endless task would keep her occupied for a while, I went on with my own chores.

"Sorry, buddy," I said to Archie, who would have loved to continue to play fetch with me. "I have work to do."

Archie settled down in front of the fireplace, and I cleaned the great hall, all the while taking notes about the furniture in the little notebook I'd brought along.

I was just dusting off a Georgian-style end table that looked interesting to me when a male voice made me wince.

"Hello!"

I turned around to see Sir Euan, bedecked in his kilt.

"Oh, hello!" I was glad to see him again. A part of me had hoped he'd finally moved on, but deep inside I'd known just discovering his grave and making him realize he was a ghost wouldn't do the trick.

"How are you, Euan?"

He frowned. "It's Sir Euan to you. Since you appear new here, however—"

"New?" I interrupted. "What do you mean? It's me, Bethany."

The lines on Euan's forehead deepened. "I'm sorry.

Have we met before? I can't be expected to remember the face of every new maid, but it seems to me that I would have remembered yours." He looked me up and down with appreciation.

My eyes went to the feather duster I was holding and then to the black dress that was, admittedly, not a great choice for cleaning chores. But my one and only pair of jeans and T-shirt, which I would have preferred to wear for this, were in the laundry. Since I'd put my hair up and covered it with a headscarf, with a big stretch of the imagination, this outfit could pass as the uniform of an early-twentieth-century maid.

That still didn't explain why Sir Euan couldn't remember me. We'd gone through what I'd thought had been a transformative event together just a few nights ago.

Had all of it been for nothing?

"Don't you remember the other night?" I asked carefully. "When I…showed you something."

"Oh!" Sir Euan winced. "I am sorry if we…made each other's acquaintance before and I don't recall. Was I intoxicated?"

When I didn't answer right away, he said, "I'm so sorry, lass. I'm sure you showed me…something marvelous." He gave me a meaningful look.

I was a bit at a loss as to how to proceed. Penny and I had made a brilliant plan, but if I had to start anew and prove to Euan that he was a ghost again… Or was that even necessary? Could I just reverse Esme's spell? Would that suffice?

"Let me make this up to you," Sir Euan said, interpreting my facial expression and my silence the wrong way. "Meet me tonight in my chamber. Let me treat you to fine wine and delicious morsels, and… I'm sure I'll never forget you again."

"Yes!" I answered enthusiastically. This would be my

chance to put my plan into action, and if I had to go through everything from the other night again, I would do that too.

Sir Euan was clearly pleased by my eagerness. "Wonderful. I'll see you tonight, Bethany."

"Until tonight."

He went out the front door, and I quickly took photos of the end table and jotted down notes before I packed up my supplies and left the castle.

"See you later, buddy," I called goodbye to Archie, who lifted his head and gave a short bark.

I had to hurry to go into town to buy cocoa, cinnamon, nutmeg, and honey.

I'd keep my promise to Hattie and bring Sir Euan his cocoa tonight.

It fit perfectly into my plan.

CHAPTER TWENTY-TWO

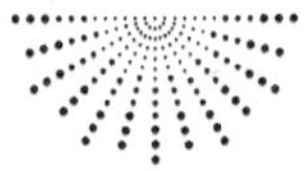

I pulled into a parking space in front of the nearest supermarket, taking deep breaths to calm my nerves.

Since I'd been fine driving Alex's car from the cottage to the castle, I'd told myself I could drive it to the store. But it wasn't quite the same thing if there were other cars taking part in the traffic and you weren't driving down a single-lane dirt road. It would take me a while to get the hang of driving on the wrong side of the road.

When my phone rang, I just picked up without paying attention to who was calling.

"Yes?"

"Bethany?"

"Mom?" Something in her tone alarmed me, and I snapped to attention. "Is everything all right?"

"Funny…" She gave a humorless laugh. "I was about to ask you the same question."

"What do you—"

"I just got off the phone with my mother. She told me she had something to do with getting you hired by this artist in Scotland. Something about a coven of *witches* who will help you develop your *gift*."

The way she emphasized some of her words left no doubt about what Mom's opinion was about the whole idea.

My mouth dried up. "So you *are* in contact with Kirsty, then?" I said weakly.

"She reaches out every once in a while, and I rarely pick up or call her back. She called me from an unknown number this time, and I didn't think. After she mentioned your name, I listened to what she had to say. Please tell me this is just one of her delusions."

Mom's voice sounded icy, but by the end of her answer, her voice trembled.

I swallowed. "It's true." Before she could interrupt, I said, "And you know it's true. I asked you if you'd ever seen ghosts, and you admitted you had."

"I said no such thing. What I meant was that, when I was younger, I sometimes saw things that weren't really there. People others didn't perceive. That's not seeing ghosts, Bethany, that's delusions. It's a mental illness. Doctors with medical degrees diagnosed your grandmother. And I told you how to deal with it so you don't have to suffer the same fate."

"You told me to ignore it completely and it would go away by itself," I said, incredulously.

"Yes, and instead you're going around telling other people, joining some sort of…whatever it is…where other women have the same delusions? By the sound of it, you're egging each other on and telling each other that you have paranormal abilities. You're doing the exact opposite of what I advised. This will not make it better. I think you should return home immediately!"

I pinched my nose. Normally, I'd make something up to get out of this kind of conversation. I'd find something that would appease my mother. Sometimes I straight-up lied to make sure I'd stay on her good side. Or so she wouldn't be disappointed in me. Anything so I wouldn't have to confront her with a different opinion.

But I could see now how immature that was. I hadn't planned on discussing this on the phone. Especially considering what my mother had been through. I wanted to talk to her in person.

"Your advice would be terrible if you really thought I was suffering from a mental illness," I said to her.

"What?"

"I don't think you do, Mom. I think you know this is about something else. But even if... Do you really believe that someone should keep their delusions or psychotic episodes to themself? Not talk to anyone about it, pretend they don't exist?"

"It worked in my case," my mother said tensely. "You just have to put your mind to it. Or do you want to end up like your grandmother? I didn't want to have this happen to you and your brother. They would have taken you away..."

She sobbed, and I just sat there in shock. I'd never heard my mother cry before. I felt awful.

"Mom," I said gently. "Even if you had sought help and it had taken you away from us, we would have been fine. We would have had Dad and our grandparents. It wouldn't have been like with you. And times have changed. There are ways to talk to someone about these things without immediately getting committed to an institution. Even that could be a good thing for people who really need it." I sighed. I was getting off track. "Anyway, the point I was trying to make is that it can't be healthy to ignore problems regarding mental health. Or anything, really. To pretend it doesn't exist and just repress it cannot be beneficial in the long term."

My mother didn't reply, but at least she'd stopped crying.

"Again, I understand you only wanted to protect me and John. It was awful what you had to go through as a child. You had no family, no support system. But this…" I didn't want to say coven. "This group of women in Tarbet is that support system for our unique abilities. And I think you know that's what it is, Mom. I absolutely get that you're scared. That's why you wanted to keep your distance from Kirsty, isn't it? So you wouldn't have to confront that part of yourself that you don't understand and that makes you similar to your mother. That you blamed it for tearing you two apart. And I'm scared too. But I also know that this gift is a part of myself that I don't want to suppress."

We stayed quiet for a long while, and just when I started to ask whether she was still there, my mother said, "Then you're a lot braver than I ever was."

"I don't know about that. I didn't have your childhood, so it's not exactly fair to compare us. And I really do love antiques, old furniture…you know, things that ghosts are attached to. It's my calling, and ignoring ghosts just wouldn't work for me. I'd really have to twist myself into being someone I'm not. Ghosts come with the territory, and I'm scared about having to deal with them. I'm trying to get one to stop haunting the castle and move on at the moment, and it's terrifying. You don't have to do the same thing. I think, with you, just acknowledging that you once had latent abilities is a start. Talking to Grandma is a start. Although I'd love for you to come to Scotland—"

"What are you talking about?" my mother interrupted, sounding almost like her old self again. "What ghost are you interacting with? That sounds really dangerous! I'm not sure you should do that, Bethany!"

I bit my lips. I had told my mother too much.

"Don't worry, Mom, this is a really friendly ghost. He, ummm, he even has a dog."

"A dog? As a ghost?"

"Yes, a little ghost doggy. It's going to be fine. Not a thing to be concerned about. I have to go now. Talk to you later!"

I hung up and made a face, sticking my tongue out at my reflection in the rearview mirror. Old habits die hard, or maybe I wasn't really as mature as I'd decided a few minutes ago.

But I only had to get this over with, finally get Euan to move on, and then I could call my mother back with a success story.

~

"ARE you sure you don't want me to come with you?" Alex asked for the hundredth time that evening, while I carefully transferred the hot chocolate into a thermos.

"You know that wouldn't be helpful. Euan needs to think I'm there for a date."

"But what if something happens—"

"We've been over this. Worst-case scenario, I'll have my phone." I held it up and put it in the basket together with the thermos and the two mugs. "Sir Euan can't really do anything to me."

I still hadn't told Alex about the outburst of rage in the graveyard, when Euan had caused the gravestones to tumble and the ground to shake in such a manner that the casket had been unearthed.

The ghost of Euan Campbell certainly had some power, and I couldn't assert with confidence that this power would not cause me harm in some way.

Euan had been angered by seeing his gravestone, though, and his wrath had been a byproduct of coming to terms with realizing he was a ghost.

I had no intention of showing Euan the graveyard today—at least, not if I could help it.

Letting Euan learn he was a ghost hadn't done the trick after all, and he'd promptly forgotten it again.

I hoped that going through all that wouldn't even be necessary. The antidote spell should work, and *then* Euan would realize that he wasn't corporeal and needed to move on.

"I'm not worried Euan will do me harm," I said to Alex with conviction. "My biggest concern is to get him to ingest the antidote. I didn't see any evidence that Sir Euan could touch material things. You know, like Hattie could carry the tray or like Archie could fetch the sponge. But Hattie says she brings him cocoa every evening, so he might be able to incorporate drinking the beverage into his plane of existence…or whatever it is."

"Would he not have a mug for that already…or is it an imaginary one?" Alex shook his head. "It's confusing. I don't quite get it."

I sighed. "Me neither. All I know is that *I* will *not* drink out of a mug that's been there for a hundred years." I shuddered, thinking about the decomposed food. I still didn't know what part of it had been real and what had been in the ghostly realm of existence.

"Do you have to drink it? With the potion Penny concocted? Isn't that dangerous? If the herbs have something to counteract atropine—"

"Digoxin," I said, closing my eyes to remember the word. "In the foxglove. It could be poisonous in its own right. And some other components in—"

I stopped talking when I opened my eyes again and saw alarm on Alex's face.

"I'm only taking a sip, if that. It's going to be fine. I trust Gillian—in my psychic vision, I could tell she wanted to make up for her fatal mistake of aiding and abetting Esme. And I trust Penny, as well. Also," I added, because Alex didn't seem particularly convinced by that, "you have to remember this isn't strictly about science. There's a spell involved."

"Hmm. Which makes everything even less certain, because you're new to this, and we have no idea what might happen."

I tried to hide my own insecurities when I put my hand on his cheek. "You can trust *me*, can't you?"

He smiled, the skin around his eyes crinkling in a very attractive fashion. "Yes. I trust you."

"I can do this."

"Okay… But call me as soon as you're done. I'll meet you halfway to the castle."

"Yes, I'll do that."

I took a step back, double-checked the contents of my basket, then smoothed down the fabric of my pale-pink-and-white-striped sundress. "Do I look okay?"

"You look beautiful." Alex's green eyes lit up, and I knew he really meant it. He clearly didn't think I was pretty in a boring way anymore. Our eyes locked, and I got butterflies in my stomach.

I blew out a breath. "I'd better go." Grabbing the basket, I gave Alex a quick kiss on the cheek. "Wish me luck."

"I'll be here, waiting for your call, and thinking about you the entire time. Good luck."

"Thanks." I rushed out the front door before I could change my mind.

I did want to do this for Euan, and I had felt pretty confident after my visit to Penny, but Alex was right. And my mother probably had a point too.

I was really new at this, and there was no telling what would happen.

CHAPTER TWENTY-THREE

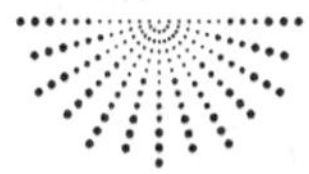

By the time I reached the castle, I was almost as nervous as on the night I'd first met Euan in his chamber.

I knew the castle better by now, but it was still spooky to go there at night, especially upstairs.

Encountering Hattie or Archie might have made me feel less alone, but I didn't see either of them.

I rushed up the spiral staircase, then hesitated in front of the oak door.

Like the times I'd stood here before, I had a weird feeling of doing something forbidden, something delicious but dangerous.

It might have had to do with Euan's ghostly energy—he was a Casanova after all, and by inviting me on this date, he'd only really had one thing in mind. And he'd been murdered. Mrs. MacDonald clearly thought the castle needed to get rid of his particular haunting energy. She'd never mentioned Hattie or Archie or other ghosts as a problem, and I certainly never got any feelings close to this when I encountered them.

Whatever it was, it just added to my trepidation.

I was close to turning around and going back to the cottage. Alex wouldn't fault me for it—he'd probably be glad I'd chickened out and hadn't gotten myself in trouble.

Alex was happy where he was. He wouldn't mind staying in the cottage and having Euan haunt the castle forever, just like it had always been.

But then I reminded myself that I'd decided part of my job description as a muse was to lead Alex to new experiences. He was stuck in a rut, burying himself in his work, not moving out of his comfort zone. It would be pretty hypocritical of me to shy away from challenges that pushed me out of my comfort zone myself.

And Penny and I had made a good plan. Everything was prepared. I also had the opportunity, since Euan had invited me here. If I didn't go through with it now, who knew if or when I'd get the chance again?

So I pulled myself together and pushed the door open.

There was the scent of roses again, like last time.

I saw the pink petals on the bed and on the floor.

The room looked just like it had the other night. There were the champagne flutes and the dishes covered in cloches on the card table.

The piano music started, and Euan Campbell appeared in front of the window.

"Bethany, my sweet muse. You came."

I closed the door behind me. "Yes." I cleared my throat. "And I brought you something."

After lifting the basket to show it to him, I set it down on the floor next to the table. I took out the thermos and the mugs, placing them on the card table.

"I made special spiced cocoa for you, since I heard you enjoy it so much."

"How sweet."

"Let me pour it for us."

"Shouldn't we have champagne first? Cocoa is more of a nightcap, don't you think? And I'm not quite ready to turn in yet."

Euan smiled seductively, but it seemed forced. He was clearly playing out this scene just like last time, and I'd interrupted the pattern.

It occurred to me that ghosts tended to do that, like Hattie with her chores and peeling the same potato again and again.

Euan had entertained so many women in this chamber, maybe he had a seduction routine down.

I finished pouring the cocoa and said, "Of course. Champagne sounds lovely."

"But first…" He held out a hand. "May I have this dance?"

I gave my own forced smile. "Sure."

His hand passed through my waist again. This time I was prepared for the feeling of being stabbed by an icicle, but I still flinched a little.

I gave my best effort to follow Sir Euan's lead and move to the music, but I was soon trying to think of an excuse to extricate myself.

Last time, Euan had seen it as a sign that he'd been too forward, and that had led to a conversation about Esme.

That wouldn't really serve my purpose today. All I wanted was for him to drink the cocoa.

A sound interrupted my thoughts.

Euan heard it too. He frowned. "What was that?"

I recognized the barking. "It's Archie. Your dog?"

"Ah, where is he? It sounds like he's outside. He shouldn't be roaming around out there at night."

He stepped away from me, and I breathed a sigh of relief. I rubbed my arms, still full of goosebumps from being chilled by his "touch."

I followed him to the window and looked down at the

moonlit graveyard. The barking definitely came from down there.

I craned my neck. "There he is. I saw movement between the graves."

"Can you open the window and call out to him to get his attention?" Euan sounded worried. "I'll get Hattie to fetch him, but I don't want him to run away in the meantime."

"Of course." I struggled with the window but then managed to open a pane. "Archie! Buddy!" I whistled. The barking stopped, and I thought I could see the dog look up at me, his tail wagging. "Stay. That's a good boy." I continued to call down to him for a little while, and when I turned around, I saw that Sir Euan was already back in the room.

"It's all right now. Hattie is on her way to get him."

"Oh, that was fast." I closed the window.

"That cocoa smells delicious. Does it have cinnamon in it?" Euan leaned over the table and inhaled the scent from the still-steaming mug.

I was surprised that, as a ghost, he could smell something on my plane of existence. But it just showed how little I knew about how ghosts interacted with the "real" world. "Yes. And nutmeg."

"Sounds perfect."

I jumped at my chance. "I'd love for you to try it."

At the table, I took a mug in each hand.

Considering how dismissive he had been about sampling his nightcap earlier, Euan seemed oddly excited about this. "Will you drink as well?"

"Of course." My smile was probably a little strained, but only because I was holding my breath.

What would happen when I gave Sir Euan the mug? Would his fingers pass straight through it, instantly chilling the drink? The mug might fall. There would be ceramic shards and cocoa everywhere, and I'd have to explain to him that it had happened because he was a ghost.

I took a deep breath, then drank a small sip of the hot chocolate. "Hmm. It's good, you really should try it."

I held out the mug to him, not letting go of it right away. Carefully, I lifted my fingers. To my amazement, the mug didn't fall prey to gravity.

It seemed as if Sir Euan was really holding it.

I let my hand drop in slow motion, ready to shoot it up again if it looked as if the mug would fall. But Euan brought it to his lips.

In order to hide the expression of relief that had to be evident on my face, I lifted my own mug and took a long sip of cocoa.

When I put it down again, Euan looked at me expectantly.

"Is it to your liking?" I asked, a little uncertain.

"Yes. It's delicious. Let's drink up."

Since I was eager for him to drink as much as possible, I complied, even though I was a little worried about ingesting so much of Penny's potion.

Truth be told, I hadn't thought about it when we'd made the plan. I'd figured I'd just pretend to drink it. Alex had raised a valid concern earlier. The herbal concoction worked as an antidote to the poisonous components in belladonna, but the ingredients were poisonous in their own right.

I was getting a little panicked. My heart rate picked up, and I didn't know if I could attribute it to anxiety—or if the potion in the cocoa was doing a number on me.

So I just pretended to drink, giving Sir Euan a chance to finish his own cup.

But when I lifted my gaze, Euan gave me a strange look again.

"Did you drink it all?"

Looking back at that moment, I could never be sure if my mug slipped accidentally through my fingers or if I did it on purpose. It might have been on my mind because I'd worried it would happen to Euan earlier. I certainly didn't want to finish the poisonous drink, and it could have been my way of making sure that I didn't have to.

The important thing at that moment was that Sir Euan had ingested the potion, and now I was eager to finish what I'd started. Nothing else mattered.

Sir Euan's reaction was so strange, however, that the words of the spell sort of stuck in my throat before I could utter them.

Instead of jumping back or being upset about the broken mug and spilled cocoa, he just looked at me with a sort of elated expression in his eyes.

"Are you feeling all right?"

I still couldn't get a word out, and now my heart really started to pound in my chest. Heat rose to my cheeks, and dizziness made me sway a little.

I shook my head. "No…" I croaked.

My distress didn't appear to worry Sir Euan. On the contrary. He seemed even more fascinated by what he was witnessing.

I wanted to grab my phone, but it was in the basket, and I suddenly realized the basket was no longer next to the table where I'd put it earlier.

My eyes went back to Euan, desperately seeking a sign of compassion or even understanding of what was happening.

"Help," I gasped, clutching my chest. "Something's wrong. I need help."

Sir Euan smiled.

"Oh, no one is going to help you now, Bethany."

It dawned on me that I'd made a fatal mistake.

I'd assumed I was doing a good thing here and that it automatically meant there would be no malintent from the ghost.

And now I was going to die.

CHAPTER TWENTY-FOUR

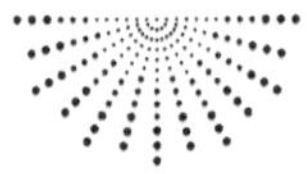

"What…what have you done?"

My throat still felt like I was choking, but I couldn't remember if that was a symptom of a plant poison I'd discussed with Penny.

Heart palpitations certainly were the first sign of atropine in the bloodstream, but I was far too panicked to go through the list of what else belladonna poisoning caused.

All I knew was that something was wrong. Very wrong.

And Euan would do nothing to help me. On the contrary, he seemed thrilled about the turn of events.

He stepped closer and looked at me with large puppy-dog eyes. "You'll forgive me, won't you? I've been alone for far too long. I don't want to be on my own anymore. A man like me isn't meant to be without a beautiful woman by his side. You'll stay on as my muse, Bethany. I need you."

I stared at him. I could hardly move a muscle; only my chest was heaving from the insane heartbeat. "You…you remembered…what happened the other night? You just pretended you didn't so you could…"

My eyes went to the puddle of cocoa on the floor. Then I shook my head slightly. "No. You couldn't. You couldn't have poisoned me."

Where would Euan even have gotten the poison from? And he wasn't capable of touching material things, actually putting poison in my mug, and mixing it in.

It had to be mistake…I was only imagining things.

Or this reaction was because of the small amount of the antidote potion I'd swallowed.

Maybe it was merely happening on Euan's plane of existence, and I was somehow caught up in it?

I was starting to feel better, convinced my mind was merely playing tricks on me, when Euan turned to the bureau and opened the little drawer.

My eyes bugged. "You can…touch things?" He'd held on to the mug, but I'd thought it had been the exception.

"I practiced." Euan sounded proud. "Actually, I've done nothing but practice since I made this decision." He pulled out the little jar.

"See, this item puzzled me when you showed it to me the other day. The drawer contained my keepsakes, things that Esme had given me." His lips stretched into a sad smile. "She'd given this to me too, in a way. It was her parting gift."

He held up the little jar. I could now see the wax seal had been broken. The jar's contents were dark but glinted golden in the light coming from the wall sconces when Euan turned the jar in his hand.

"It's the honey Esme used to sweeten my spiced cocoa on the night I died. A special heather honey from her village, she'd claimed. I wondered why she'd resealed it and left it here, in the drawer only she and I knew about. It was just like Esme to do something like that. Risking someone finding it, tempting fate. Leaving it as evidence of the revenge she'd exacted on me—no doubt what she'd called a sweet revenge."

I felt the blood drain out of my face, suddenly feeling not flushed but ice cold.

The honey contained the belladonna poison.

And Euan must have drawn the same conclusion. He'd added some of it to the cocoa when I'd been distracted—the barking in the graveyard and Euan instructing me to keep Archie's attention on me! Euan had probably not even left the room to get Hattie, but rather had used the time I'd been preoccupied with the dog to poison the cocoa.

That thought made me feel even worse. Had he enlisted Archie in his scheme? I'd thought the ghost dog and I were becoming friends, and now Archie had played a part in my…murder.

No! I couldn't let this happen. I couldn't let myself be murdered by a ghost. It would destroy my mother.

Trying to keep calm so my heart rate wouldn't speed up anymore, I said to Euan, "So you remember everything from that last night, then? What Esme did?"

"Yes. I should have known something was wrong because she'd been very prickly with me for a while. Whenever I caught her alone, she'd just remind me of my promise, insisting I'd do the honorable thing. That night, though, she gave me a sweet embrace. It was as it had been before. Call me a fool, but I thought Esme had finally seen reason. But I should have known. She was too sweet…"

A sad expression crossed his face when his gaze moved to the jar he'd put on top of the bureau. "Too sweet like the honey, masking the taste of bitter poison." He shook his head. "She even recited a poem. She must have read it somewhere and memorized it just for the occasion. Like I told you, Esme wasn't a wordsmith. I should have known she was only playing a part, that her wish to reunite wasn't genuine."

"A poem? Do you remember it?"

He waved it off. "It wasn't very good. Like what a young lass might come up with. Something about sleep and cherries."

I immediately thought of the devil's cherry. It must have been the spell. If I made it out of here alive, Penny and I would have to find it in the grimoire.

But to do that, I needed to work a little magic of my own first.

My spell had been meant for Sir Euan, to counteract what Esme had done to him, so he could finally find eternal rest.

But it was also an antidote to belladonna poisoning. It might help me—if I hurried. I could only hope I wasn't too late.

"I have something I want to say myself," I said, panting a little. My breath was coming too fast. "A toast. To us staying together forever." I unscrewed the thermos and poured a little cocoa in the empty champagne flutes. I really had to concentrate because my hand shook and I was feeling dizzy.

Euan looked at me in surprise. "You'll agree to it?"

I nodded weakly, focusing on picking up the flutes. "I wish you'd asked. I would have liked to have a choice in this—"

"I didn't think you'd readily agree." Euan came closer. "But…then again, I knew we had a special connection. You feel it too?"

"Of course. I'd never seen a ghost before you…maybe I was just meant to see *you*. Besides," I tried a smile, "what more could a girl wish for than to stay forever by the side of the handsome lord of a castle? I've dreamed of being a princess. Now it's coming true. It's like a fairy-tale ending. Happily ever after."

I lay all the conviction of my former self into this speech, the naive girl I'd been just a week ago, when I'd come over to Scotland with hopes and dreams I could hardly relate to anymore.

Euan had to feel there was truth to what I was saying. If he got suspicious of how easily I was complying, he wouldn't play along, and my plan wouldn't work out.

"Yes," Euan said happily. "You're my princess. Forever."

"So let's celebrate." I passed him a flute.

I had to suppress a jubilant scream when he actually grabbed it, held it up, and clinked it against mine.

I quickly recited the spell:

Yarrow and hemlock to find peace,
Add foxglove for sweet release,
Reverse the dark, restore the light,
A final kiss will end this plight

Euan had frowned at what I was saying, but when I leaned forward and planted a kiss on his ice-cold lips, his worries appeared to abate.

"Bethany, my sweet muse, I—"

He stopped talking, seemingly aware of something behind me.

"What's this?"

I turned around but couldn't see anything.

Instead, my attention shifted to the fact that I instantly felt better. The herbal concoction, which had already been in the cocoa when I'd brought it along, must have been working against the atropine in the belladonna.

Or maybe it really was the spell.

In any case, I hoped that I'd be okay until I could get myself to the emergency room, at least.

Euan clearly felt different too.

"What's happening to me?" he asked, looking at his arms and hands. They were ever-so-slightly see-through, as if his corporeal form was dissolving. "Why am I so… light?"

"You're floating!" I gasped, staring at his feet hovering a few inches off the floor.

A mix of emotions registered on Euan's face. "What did you do?"

I sighed. "I can't die and live as a ghost by your side, Euan. I'm meant to live. And you…you were meant to move on. Esme put on a spell on you, causing you to die a horrible, traumatic death, preventing you from finding peace. I reversed that spell. I'm sorry to disappoint you, since you wanted something else. But trust me, this is better. You'll get to find eternal rest in the place where you're meant to be."

If he'd been a little shocked by my duplicity, and probably disappointed that I wasn't going to be joining him, he was getting over it fast.

"I didn't harm you, did I?"

"You almost did. But it's okay now."

"Good, because you're right. I can see it now." He floated a little higher, turned a tad more see-through, his gaze directed at the point behind my shoulder. "I know where I'm supposed to go. Thank you, Bethany."

And with those words, he just…disappeared.

I sat there, a little stunned.

Somewhere in the back of my mind I realized I should probably call Alex so he could drive me to the hospital.

But I needed a few moments to process what had happened and to return to reality…my reality.

Everything in the room faded to the way it had always

looked in my time, or on my plane of existence, or whatever you'd call it.

Muted colors, rotting fabrics, collapsed furniture, everything covered in dust and dirt. There were the mug and the champagne flutes on the card table and the thermos with the rest of the cocoa.

No covered dishes, no gramophone playing, no rose petals on the floor.

The only thing out of the ordinary was my broken mug with the spilled cocoa.

And the little jar of honey on top of the bureau.

The atmosphere in the room had changed remarkably, though.

It was just an old room in a castle now.

It held no more ghostly secrets.

I packed up my things, taking the jar of honey as well, so I could have it analyzed.

After opening the oak door and stepping onto the spiral staircase, I turned around, giving the room a last look of goodbye.

I knew it wouldn't be calling me anymore.

CHAPTER TWENTY-FIVE

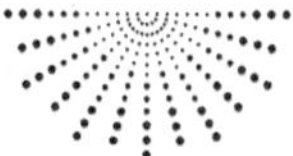

A FEW MONTHS LATER

"And this is the Euan Campbell room," I said proudly, concluding the tour of the castle.

Mrs. MacDonald had decided to turn the castle into a B&B, and I hadn't just been in charge of restoring furniture to sell in order to fund the renovations, but I'd also helped with the interior design of the rooms.

This was the room I'd struggled most with.

There wasn't a trace of Euan's spirit left, neither here nor in the rest of the old building. Everyone who'd visited the castle before confirmed that it felt quite different now. Some people, I'd learned, were more receptive to ghostly activities than others, but most had felt a dark, oppressive atmosphere before. One of Alex's relatives had asked if we'd cut down trees surrounding the castle because it felt like there was much more light.

I had seen Euan's ghost move on, and I knew there wasn't a residual of haunting energy left.

Still, I'd had some intense experiences in this room. I'd almost been murdered by a ghost. Part of me had just wanted to turn the interior into something else, completely changed from what it had looked like before, banishing everything that reminded me of Euan Campbell and what had happened here.

Talking my experiences over with Mrs. MacDonald and my grandmother had made me realize, though, that you couldn't expect ghosts to behave like living beings. Of course, the actions of the living rarely made logical sense either. Things were rarely black and white, and even though Sir Euan had done something bad to me, it didn't mean he'd been a malicious ghost.

He'd been bespelled and made to suffer, and in me, he'd seen a light. Something soothing that promised the end of his suffering. That's what my gift was to ghosts, after all. He'd interpreted it the wrong way, hadn't known what I could truly do for him, had just wanted me to be his companion in death.

Sure, he'd had his faults. Euan hadn't done right by Esme MacDonald, and the spurned maid had made him pay for it terribly.

But don't we all have our character flaws?

And we all just long for the same things, no matter what twisted ways we go about getting them: love and acceptance.

In the end, I'd figured if Mrs. MacDonald could forgive him, so could I.

I'd been so nervous about telling her what her mother had done. I'd even asked Penny to come along as moral support. But in true Mrs. MacDonald fashion, the coven leader hadn't even seemed surprised. She might have known all along, although probably not in detail. She'd certainly seemed sad when I'd told her about Sir Euan waking up in the casket, realizing he'd been buried alive, only to perish for real this time.

Through a conversation with my grandmother, I had learned that I could bring ghosts and their loved ones together. Most people weren't able to see and talk to the ghosts like we did, but with a bit of effort, there could be a connection, and sometimes even communication of a sort.

I'd asked Mrs. MacDonald if she would have wanted to meet her father before he'd moved on. Clearly, she wasn't an ordinary person, and if anyone could communicate with beings from another plane of existence, it was probably her. Besides, from what I'd heard about the coven activities, it should have been possible to allow Mrs. MacDonald to talk to her father.

"Euan Campbell may have sired me, but I don't consider him my father," had been Mrs. MacDonald's answer. "Don't get me wrong, I'm glad he's found peace. But I didn't want to have anything to do with it. I just needed to have the energy of the terrible things my mother had done cleared out of the castle. Besides," she'd given me one of her mysterious smiles, "that wasn't so much about me and my past but more about you and your future, Bethany."

Where the room renovation was concerned, I'd eventually decided that it would be right to pay tribute to Euan. He'd been the last lord of the castle, and this had been his private chamber—a place that had clearly meant a lot to him.

The room was restored to its former glory, with the mahogany bed and bureau refinished. I'd found fabric like the one that had deteriorated over the years, so the red-and-gold carpets, drapes, and bedspreads shone in splendor.

I'd even put information about Euan Campbell on a laminated card in the welcome pack for guests on the little card table.

Looking at the room now, I felt satisfied but also a little sad that my work here was done. Mrs. MacDonald didn't plan on running the B&B herself—she needed to stay in Tarbet—and Alex and I were busy with our own careers.

So Mrs. MacDonald had hired a manager to take care of the day-to-day of the B&B. I'd already offered to help out, though, since the castle meant a lot to me, and I liked to spend time in it.

It was opening weekend, and we had some very special guests I was showing around.

My mother and my grandmother.

I was so happy that Mom and I had reconnected with Grandma. I'd spoken on the phone with Kirsty a lot in recent months, but this was the first time we were meeting in person.

Three months ago, I'd been able to get away for a quick trip to the US, but mainly to spend some quality time with my mother and talk about everything.

My mother had come a long way, even though she still had trouble accepting her gift. At least she seemed to believe Grandma and I could communicate with ghosts, so that was something.

The main thing was that she'd been much more relaxed and happier since she had a relationship with Grandma again.

Since I first laid eyes on Kirsty today, I'd had a hard time not staring at her. I still couldn't get over how different she looked from the old, confused, anguished lady I'd always imagined her to be.

I'd forgotten that she'd had my mother young, and really, they looked like sisters, especially since they'd gotten matching haircuts.

Kirsty had been through very tough times in her life, which you could still tell from the many lines around her mouth and eyes, but my grandmother also possessed a spark that made up for it.

"You've done a wonderful job with this B&B." Kirsty complimented me as we walked down the stairs back to the lobby.

"Thank you." I beamed even more when my mother readily agreed. I was so used to her more passive-aggressive old self that I still found it a little hard to adjust.

"And I don't just mean the furniture," Kirsty added. "As far as I can tell, the castle is almost ghost-free. I know what it's like to come to terms with this ability and then accept it and help ghosts move on without having any guidance. From what you told me about Sir Euan, it couldn't have been easy. You did well. And you know, in the future you can always call me. I feel I'm still new at this myself." She smiled. "But I'd do anything I can to help you."

"Thanks, Grandma." I squeezed her arm. "You said *almost* ghost-free…You mean Archie, don't you?"

My mother looked around uncertainly. "Who's Archie?"

"Remember the…umm, little doggy I told you about?" I looked behind me at the huge gray beast that trotted down the stairs after us, wagging his tail. I wasn't sure if my grandmother could see him.

"I convinced Hattie to follow Sir Euan, but Archie…he should follow his master, shouldn't he?"

"Oh yes, pets go where their master goes," Kirsty answered. "Usually their souls stay on earth until the master dies too, and then they move on when he or she dies. It's no surprise Archie's ghost stayed here since Euan, his master, was not ready to move on."

"So what's the problem, then?" I frowned. "Archie should have followed Euan."

My grandmother chuckled. "If he hadn't found a new human, he would have."

"A new human?" My eyes widened with understanding. "Me?"

Kirsty nodded.

"Oh no!" I put my hand over my mouth. "Now he has to stay here with me?"

"It's not a bad thing. Animal ghosts can be quite happy on earth, like I said. He'll be glad to go wherever you go."

My mother, now visibly more relaxed, laughed. "I envy you, Bethany. I wouldn't mind a little ghost pet."

My grandmother and I exchanged a knowing look and grinned. So Gran could see Archie after all.

We'd arrived in the lobby—formerly the big hall where I'd found the Chesterfield suite—and ended our chat. Everything was ready for the official B&B opening, which was also a first viewing of some of Alex's new sculptures.

I didn't know which I was prouder of—that I'd done so well with the furniture in the castle or that I'd inspired Alex in his American Venus series.

His new work really was amazing I thought, not for the first time, as my eyes fell on one of the sculptures in the hall. Alex had made the stone come alive, and most of the guests marveled at the female figures.

A server was going around with a tray full of glasses of champagne, and I grabbed a glass just as Alex appeared by my side.

"There you are." He seemed really nervous. His cheeks were flushed, and his dark curls stuck out every which way.

"I wanted to show my mom and Grandma the castle," I said. "Sorry you had to wait for me."

I knew Alex was supposed to give a speech. Mrs. MacDonald had asked him to, since she didn't feel comfortable speaking in front of so many people.

"You're not anxious about your speech, are you?" I asked, a little surprised. He hadn't let on that it was worrying him.

"No, it's not that…"

"Oh, everyone loves your sculptures," I said, thinking that it had to be about showcasing his recent work. After the trials and tribulations with his art in the last years, he was probably feeling insecure.

"I know. I'm not really thinking about that right now."

I frowned. "What are you thinking about then?"

"You."

Before I could ask any further questions, Alex went a few steps up the stairs and asked for everyone's attention.

People stopped chatting and turned toward him.

I couldn't help but feel a sense of pride. This was my boyfriend!

Alex looked splendid in his Campbell kilt, his masculine body filling out the traditional outfit nicely. His hair was a little long, but I liked it when his curls went wild. Even though his moss-green eyes sometimes reminded me of his ancestor Euan, there was usually a different, more earnest expression in them. And his face was just so handsome.

I tried to calm myself down and told myself to stop gazing at him admiringly, being so obvious in front of all these people.

Alex thanked everyone for coming.

"This is a very special evening for me, and not only because we're reopening the Campbell estate to the public, so to speak. This castle has been dark and empty for far too long, a wonderful heritage site left to crumble to pieces. Nobody likes to talk about it, but keeping a historical building like this alive costs a lot of money. I'm not sure if it was a stroke of luck or genius that my Aunt Mary MacDonald brought Bethany Prince to us. Bethany only graduated last year with a degree in art history, but she specializes in furniture, and she has a fantastic eye for antiques. She identified valuable items and had them restored, helping my aunt raise enough money to renovate the castle. She even managed to refurbish it on a budget so that we could turn it into a B&B, keeping the integrity of this place intact while continually raising money to keep up with repairs. Some rooms are actually furnished as they would have been during the time the last occupant, Sir Euan Campbell, was still alive. To sum up, we wouldn't be standing here if it weren't for Bethany's hard work and ingenuity. I think this deserves a round of applause. Bethany?"

Alex beckoned me over, and everyone clapped.

Heat rose to my cheeks. I'd had no idea that I'd feature so prominently in Alex's speech, and I was a little embarrassed.

But he clearly wanted me to step up next to him, and I couldn't refuse. Besides, the least I could do was stand by his side to give him confidence. He still seemed more nervous than I'd ever seen him before.

I went up the steps and squeezed his arm before turning to the crowd. "Thanks," I mumbled.

"Now, as lovely as it is to see this castle in all its splendor, some of you know me well enough to realize that running a B&B isn't my calling."

Some people laughed at that.

"But it was Aunt Mary's dream, which is coming true long after she successfully fought for this rightful inheritance of hers. And I owe Mary MacDonald a lot. She has always believed in me and supported my work. Even when times were tough. When she suggested hiring a muse to inspire my art, I couldn't refuse. Even though I would have liked to, since the idea seemed just a little crazy to me."

More laughs.

"It was a good thing I trusted my aunt, because it worked. This evening is special to me too, because it's the first time I'm showing some of my new sculptures from the American Venus series. There will be an exhibition in Glasgow later this year. This wouldn't have been possible without Bethany, my muse. With what I can only call a baffling and mysterious foresight, my aunt sent just the right woman to my doorstep. Bethany rescued this castle, and she rescued my career. She also rescued me. I'm deeply grateful to her."

Alex turned to me with love in his eyes.

Everyone clapped again, and I was so deeply embarrassed by now that my face had to be bright red.

I didn't know what to think. Yes, I'd played a big part in financing the castle restoration and in overseeing the interior design of the B&B. Since this was the grand opening, I guessed it was okay to mention the part I had in it.

And it *was* the first time Alex was displaying some of his most recent sculptures, and they were no doubt masterpieces. I felt I had some part in that too.

But the castle was still Mrs. MacDonald's vision, and the art Alex's work. I might have been flattered had he mentioned me at the start of his big exhibition. But why place so much emphasis on me here, now? Something about it wasn't sitting right with me.

When Alex went down on one knee, it suddenly fell into place. I knew where this was heading.

"Bethany, I couldn't think of a better evening than this one, which represents everything I'm so thankful to you for, to ask you a very important question. Do you want to be my wife?"

I stood there, like a deer in the headlights for a moment, staring at the red garnet engagement ring.

Inexplicably, what went through my head at that moment was that Alex could never afford a ring like that and that it had to be an heirloom.

Probably from Mrs. MacDonald, who had given him the ring so he could propose to me today.

I tore my gaze away and searched the crowd with panicked eyes.

I didn't miss that some people looked uncomfortable and some even concerned.

Mine wasn't the stereotypical reaction from an ecstatic fiancée-to-be.

"Bethany?" Alex whispered, with heartbreaking disbelief and desperation in his voice. He was still kneeling there, on the step, holding up the ring.

My eyes finally found Mrs. MacDonald, surrounded by Penny, Jem, Fionna, and other witches of the Tarbet coven.

She hadn't changed into more cheerful—or cleaner—attire for the occasion but wore her usual old-fashioned baggy black dress. Her dark hair was a mess, and she had uneven red lipstick on her lips. When she smiled at me, I could see red smears on her teeth too. The Tarbet coven leader gave a sort of regal nod, as if to say: it's okay, you may say yes. It's what's supposed to happen. I orchestrated it so. Remember, I told you, this has all been about your future.

It was too much.

I didn't want to hurt Alex, but he never should have done this in front of all these people.

Knowing that I wouldn't be able to do the right thing if I looked at him again, I just kept my eyes on the floor as I ran down the steps and barged through the crowd. "Excuse me," I mumbled.

Tears were clouding my vision now, and it was a miracle I even made it to the door.

But somehow I made it outside.

CHAPTER TWENTY-SIX

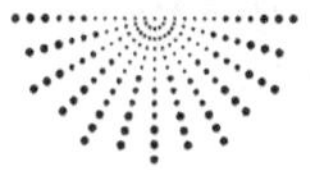

Outside, I tried to breathe in the fresh winter air, but my chest was too tight.

Panicked, I ran past the castle along a path that was no longer overgrown. Mrs. MacDonald had hired a landscaper who'd taken care of the grounds, including the graveyard. It now looked once more as if no grave had been disturbed for the last hundred years.

I hardly noticed that now, though, as I whizzed past it, trying to put as much distance as I could between me and the castle.

I ran all the way to the shore of Loch Creran, where I had to stop to catch my breath.

I wiped the tears from my eyes and was caught off guard by the breathtaking view of the wintery loch surrounded by the snow-capped mountains of Glencoe.

It didn't seem real, in a way. A romanticized version of Scotland, too picture-postcard perfect.

That made it fitting scenery for the jarring experience just now.

My stay here, in Scotland, had thrown me off course. It had been transformative, learning about a gift I'd otherwise ignored, a calling that was so much a part of my identity. It had been tough and unexpected, but it had also been amazing.

I'd been given wonderful career opportunities, had inspired an artist to create masterpieces, and in the process, I'd met my Prince Charming.

Alex falling in love with me had been the cherry on top of the icing on the cake.

Or so I'd thought.

I should have known it was all too good to be true, too close to the naive fantasies I'd dreamed up on my way over to Scotland.

I should be glad Mrs. MacDonald had cooked up this proposal only months after Alex and I had met, because I might have caught on to things much later otherwise.

"Bethany?"

Alex's voice made me spin around.

He approached me with caution, unable to meet my eyes.

When he held up my coat, I noticed how freezing it was. "I thought you might be cold," he said, passing it to me.

"Thank you," I whispered, draping the warm tweed fabric over my shoulders.

We stayed silent for a few minutes.

"I guess I owe you an explanation for…" I trailed off, not sure how to finish the sentence. Leaving you hanging? Embarrassing you in front of everyone like that? Breaking your heart?

Alex shook his head, giving me a sad smile.

"I just… I'd like to understand. I thought we loved each other and that we were happy. I thought…I thought you'd want this."

I sighed. "If you'd told old Bethany, pre-Scotland, that I'd turn down your proposal, she wouldn't have understood it either. And yes, we are in love, and we were…are happy. But it's much too soon. We've only known each other for a few months."

I wrapped my arms around myself, pulling the coat closed, and turned to the loch.

"That can't be the entire reason." Alex knew me too well. "If you really felt like that, you'd have said yes and talked to me in private about it afterward, convinced me that we should have a long engagement."

He stepped closer, and I forced myself to look him in the eyes.

"The speech you made before you proposed was all about how much you owe me and how grateful you are to me. I don't want you to marry me out of some sense of obligation."

Alex's eyes widened. "That's what you think? But it's not true. I owe you so much, and I am grateful, but I love you, and—"

"You may not know it," I interrupted him, "but your aunt cleverly made you invite me here, then made you give me a second chance so that eventually you accepted me as your muse. As the person who rescued your career. Who rescued *you*. That's what you said, isn't it?"

He wanted to protest, but I didn't let him interrupt me.

"Because your work is your life. That's what you once said. Your work is you. You're confusing your gratitude and all the feelings you have for me as your muse with love. And it's convenient. Mrs. MacDonald made it convenient. She wanted this to happen. I feel like we're marionettes on her strings."

Alex hung his head.

Then he did something very unexpected.

He laughed.

I stepped back, a little affronted. Did he think playing with our hearts like that was funny?

"You've got it completely backward, Beth. Everything."

I crossed my arms. "Really? Explain it to me, then."

"I didn't fall in love with you because you were my muse and improved my art. My proposal isn't some twisted way of thanking you for that. I created these great works of art *because* I fell in love with you. Your presence in my life made me live again, to the fullest. And that's reflected in my work."

I didn't say anything for a moment as I thought about people's responses to the sculptures tonight. I'd heard them say the sculptures were full of life, and I had to agree. So perhaps Alex was telling the truth.

"Maybe," I conceded. "But it all happened because Mrs. MacDonald wanted me here. She needed me—she told me that herself. Things always work out the way she intends them to. You know that. She wanted me to fall in love with you, and marry you, and be connected to the coven, and stay in Scotland—"

"So what?"

"Huh?"

"So what if she wanted this to happen? You want to break up and kill our happiness and not be with the person you're meant to be with just to spite my aunt? So it won't come true the way she wanted it?"

"No, that's not it. I just feel you were manipulated into asking me to marry you, and that's not a good enough reason to say yes to your proposal."

Alex thought for a moment. Then he said, "I didn't tell anyone I planned to propose. My aunt never so much as mentioned it in passing in any of our conversations."

"Didn't she give you the ring?"

Alex shook his head. "It was my grandmother's. My mom gave it to me on her deathbed."

"Oh."

"And I think you've got that backward too, by the way.

It might seem as if Mary MacDonald is orchestrating things because they work out the way she foresees them to happen. But I think it's just because she knows."

"Knows what?"

Alex shrugged. "Everything. The future."

"You mean she's such an amazing clairvoyant that she knows what's going to unfold? So it just looks like she manipulated it?"

"I think so."

I thought about all the interactions I'd had with her, and with the coven. My shoulders slumped. "You might be right. But she did put in an effort to get my mom here, and when that didn't work, she tried to get me to come to Scotland—successfully. She had her hand in it, somehow."

"And aren't you glad she did?"

Of course I was glad. If Mrs. MacDonald hadn't lured me here, I wouldn't have embraced my unique gift. I wouldn't become the person I was meant to grow into. I let out a long exhale, looking at my beautiful surroundings. The lake, the mountains, the castle…Alex. This was my home now, and I loved it.

I beamed. "Yes, I am."

Alex went down to his knee again.

I groaned. "No, wait—"

"You can say no, Beth. It will not deter me. You have to admit we're happy and that we have a great partnership. You want to stay together, don't you?"

I looked into my heart. "Yes. I want to have a real relationship, though, not a fairy-tale one. I don't know if I want to get married yet."

Alex didn't get up. "I want that too. And I love you so much I'm sure that marriage is the right thing." He held up the ring again. "You can take as much time as you need to set a wedding date, but this is my promise to you. Whenever you think is the right time to tie the knot, I'll be there. Do you accept it?"

With his words, all my worries lifted away, and I felt a million times lighter.

I smiled down at Alex.

"Yes. I do."

HEX MARKS THE COTTAGE

A Scottish Witches Mystery Short Story

1

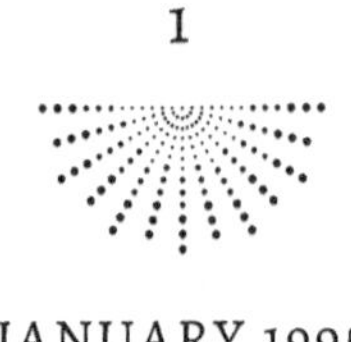

JANUARY 1995

Penny closed her eyes and listened.

The noise had stopped. Maybe her father had finally passed out.

Usually he could control himself somewhat, so that the drinking sessions with his friends on the surrounding farms didn't get completely out of hand. Officially, these visits were part of his job as a salesperson for agricultural products. While he got orders from his friends sometimes, her father hadn't been able to provide financially for his family in a while.

For two years after Penny's mother had died they'd gotten by. There might have been money in the bank to fall back on, but that was long gone. At not even sixteen years old, Penny had dropped out of school to get a job at a plant nursery.

She was earning enough for the Reid family to get by, but Penny would rather have saved up all her money. She wanted to add what she could to her nest egg so she could get a place of her own. No matter how bad things got, she never let her father persuade her to let the family use the small inheritance her mother had left her.

That inheritance was her only hope for independence, and on some days it was all she had to hold on to.

She hoped her father would pull himself together to make enough of a living if she, Penny, wasn't in the picture and it was only him and Declan.

Her father loved Penny's little brother.

Declan was five years Penny's junior and most likely the sole reason their father hadn't descended into heavy alcoholism yet. Even if he stayed out all night, he could be relied upon to get up in the morning to make his son breakfast and to be there in the afternoon when Declan got back from school.

If he drank during the day, it was never so much that Declan would notice. Their father would prepare an evening meal before he set off "to work."

Declan was involved in a lot of after-school activities, like the chess club and rugby, so he was always busy and had a lot of friends.

Tonight he was staying over at a friend's house, which was probably the reason their father hadn't exercised his usual restraint.

He certainly didn't care what Penny thought of him or what trouble he caused her.

On her good days, Penny gave him the benefit of the doubt. With her wavy golden hair, green eyes, and stunning features, she looked exactly her mother. Penny had even inherited her mother's knack for herbs and plants—along with some other more supernatural abilities her father knew nothing about. Perhaps it was too painful for her father to be reminded of his late wife.

It could be that her father blamed Penny for her mother's death. Even as a child, Penny couldn't hold her tongue when her jealous father controlled his wife. She'd certainly encouraged her mom to defy him when he'd forbidden his wife to leave the house or meet up with friends.

In her darkest hours, Penny herself wondered if she'd driven her mother to seek another way out—to get away from her abusive husband forever—by eating poisonous mushrooms.

There was comfort in the thought that her father had reasons for disliking her.

The truth was, though, that he'd never shown any love for her and had always treated her with contempt.

Penny sighed, trying to banish the thoughts. She knew there was no point trying to find rhyme or reason for her father's behavior, yet she couldn't help ruminating on it.

Ordinarily, she just put her headphones over her ears, turned the Discman on full volume, and tried to ignore her father. But tonight was different. She had to listen to the din of a drunken person stumbling around in the house, waiting for it to be over so she could get back to the task at hand.

It was that special time between the years, and her mother had taught her the ancient Celtic tradition of burning herbs during those twelve nights between Christmas and the sixth of January. She'd shown Penny methods of divination, for these nights lend themselves to finding closure with the past and looking to the future, specifically the coming year.

Penny was determined to uphold her mother's traditions, so these nights and their rituals were important to her.

She got up to open the door and listen. The house was dark and quiet. Satisfied, she locked the door and sat on the floor in front of the low table.

Penny struck a match and held it against the piece of coal until an orange flash flickered on the black surface. She blew on the coal until there was an orange glow throughout. She put a small piece of incense resin on top. Then she sprinkled a mixture of herbs over it.

The sweet, acrid smell of incense filled her nostrils, and she breathed it in slowly, until she could detect the subtler notes of juniper, lavender, and rosemary.

Penny gently fanned the smoke with the large feather of a golden eagle until the gray haze stretched to all corners of the room. All the while, Penny quietly muttered the spells her mother had taught her as a child.

Eventually, she leaned against the back of the futon and closed her eyes to meditate.

When she felt simultaneously grounded and light, she took a deep breath and opened her eyes to look into the flame of the lit candle in the middle of the table.

She grabbed the bundle of purple velvet and reverently unwrapped the fabric to reveal a deck of cards.

Penny spread the cards out on the table and moved them around.

The cards had belonged to her mother and—so she'd been told—her grandmother before that. Penny didn't even know how many generations they had been passed down. They were only used during these nights.

As a small child, Penny had begged her mother to let her play with them. The usually gentle woman had always strictly denied her request. Penny hadn't even been allowed to just look at the cards in order. She had no idea what some of the cards were. There might still be illustrations she'd never seen—and perhaps one of them would reveal itself tonight.

Penny felt the tingle of anticipation.

When she finally turned over a hitherto unfamiliar card, she wasn't even surprised. Fascinated, she looked at the illustration.

It was a traditional Highland cottage with a thatched roof. The walls were rubble stones covered in ivy and climbing roses. A black cat sat in front of the door.

In the foreground, hidden among garden plants, were bottles and jars.

Penny usually noted down impressions she got from the cards in a notebook. Each of the nights between the years corresponded with a month in the coming year. It was fun to look back at what she'd written in the notebook and see if it had come true.

Often, the interpretations were intuitive. A path and a walking stick, for example, could indicate an upcoming journey—real or metaphorical.

Animals and plants were symbolic, and her mother had taught Penny what they meant.

Tonight, though, she wasn't scribbling away in her notebook. She was at a loss as to what this cottage was supposed to represent.

A cat usually stood for independence—and Penny certainly craved that.

A cottage was a home.

But Penny hardly dared bring those ideas together and rejoice over the implications. Because that would mean her wildest dreams would come true in June this year. She feared her intense wish was father to the thought. Anyway, this cottage didn't look like what she had in mind. She was eighteen, not eighty.

And what did the bottles in the front of the illustration have to do with any of it? Were they maybe indicating that her father would stop drinking? But they looked more like apothecary bottles or jars and bottles for making preserves and syrups. They contributed to her feeling that a grandmother should reside in this cottage.

Sighing, she opened her notebook and wrote a detailed description of the card, leaving out her wild guesses.

As she put the cards and the ingredients for the ritual away, she couldn't help but feel a little annoyed.

Maybe she hadn't been in the right frame of mind after

her father had disturbed her, after all. But she didn't really want to blame him or waste more emotional energy on him.

She'd either picked the right card or not—and all would be revealed in June next year.

2

JUNE 1996

Penny slammed on the brakes when she saw the sign.

Her old car came to a screeching halt. Luckily, there wasn't much traffic on the road connecting Arrochar to Tarbet this time of day.

She pulled over to the side of the road and stared at the sign.

Cottage for Sale was all it said, beside the logo of the real estate agent and a telephone number.

Penny looked around but couldn't see any buildings close by. There was a narrow dirt track half hidden behind tall grass and shrubs.

Penny bravely turned onto the track, holding her breath in hopes that her car would make it across the uneven terrain. But only the entrance to the dirt road was a problem, almost as if nature had tried to hide it.

Penny passed a field and then a small wooded area. When the trees thinned out, she could see a dilapidated stone cottage in the distance.

Her heart raced as she parked the car in front of the cottage and got out.

Up close, the building seemed in even worse condition. Penny tried to peer through the windows, but the glass panes were so dirty she couldn't see anything. The front door was locked.

Ducking her head under low-hanging branches, she rounded the cottage. There had once been a path leading to the back, but it was overgrown now, and she could barely get through.

Circumnavigating stinging nettles and thorns, she finally made it to the other side. When she looked up, her breath caught in her throat.

The garden was vast and stretched out across various levels. A section in the back seemed to be what remained of a large rose garden.

Although the flower beds had been neglected for a while, Penny could still see that some had been used for kitchen herbs and others for flowers.

There was a marvelous array of plants that had been left to their own devices and spread all across the garden.

Like a sleepwalker, she followed old and overgrown paths meandering through the garden. Eventually, Penny arrived at a large wooden garden shed.

Penny could hardly breathe. Her whole body was covered in goosebumps.

She could feel that this garden was special, and she had the powerful impression that there was something in the shed she was supposed to see. As if she had some sort of magical connection to this place.

She couldn't explain it, since she'd felt nothing like it before. But she followed her intuition and opened the door.

To her disappointment, there wasn't much more to see than dirt and dust. She waved her hands to get rid of the cobwebs stretching from wall to wall.

There was one minor consolation: Instead of the musty

smell one might have expected in an old shed, there was the delicious fragrance of herbs in the air.

When her eyes had adjusted to the semi-darkness, Penny couldn't see any bundles of herbs hanging from the ceiling. But she was sure they had been there once upon a time.

She also imagined the large wooden table in the middle of the shed had been used to process herbs and plants.

There was an old Welsh dresser with kitchen cabinets against one wall. When Penny investigated it, she discovered a few old empty bottles and glass jars as well as a stone pestle and mortar.

She moved toward a corner partitioned off with a wooden screen. Bending to peer at the faded images, Penny could make out lifelike illustrations of plants and animals.

She moved the screen a bit to get a better look at what was behind it. To her amazement, the partition hid an old bathtub with claw feet.

The sight brought a smile to Penny's face.

She left the shed and wandered the garden for a good half an hour. She just couldn't get enough of the sight and smell of the plants.

Following an impulse, she tried the back door of the cottage. It opened.

With bated breath, she stepped inside.

It was clear that nobody had lived in this house for a long while. It was dirty and in dire need of repair. But Penny didn't mind that. It still looked wonderful to her, and she knew she had to have it.

Didn't it match the mysterious card she'd drawn at the beginning of the year, on the night that corresponded to June?

It was June now, and she had found this cottage!

Granted, the illustration had been much nicer, but

Penny could restore it to look like that. She was sure this was her rose cottage.

Aside from worrying about her brother's welfare, there was another reason Penny hadn't moved out of her family home yet: her mother's garden. It contained everything she needed for her herb spells, and she still felt close to her mother there. Neither her father nor Declan ever went there, so it was also a refuge.

This huge garden was a perfect replacement. And it was secluded, so nobody would see what she was doing.

It had to make the property valuable, though. Penny worried whether she could even afford it. She should probably be thankful the cottage was in such disrepair, which surely had to bring the price down.

She took a rosebud from the garden as a souvenir and then went back to her car. She drove up to the sign and made a note of the real estate agent's phone number.

Back home, she thanked her stars that Declan and her dad weren't home yet. She picked up the receiver and dialed the number she'd jotted down.

When someone named Irene picked up, she introduced herself.

"I'm interested in the secluded cottage between Arrochar and Tarbet. The one with the enormous garden."

"Really?" Irene said.

"Can you tell me the asking price?"

It was the exact amount of money her mother had left her.

Could there be any more signs that the cottage was hers?

"I'll take it!" she cried.

The real estate agent laughed, but not condescendingly. "Officially, that's the offer-over price, which means we're accepting offers over that asking price."

"Oh," Penny said, a little deflated.

"But don't worry, I don't mind letting you know we don't expect the price to go up much higher. You need to have a solicitor formally note your interest, and then I'll send you the home report."

"Okay." Penny actually knew a solicitor—he was a friend of someone in her coven, and he'd already dealt with her mother's inheritance. So after she'd given Irene all her details, she called the solicitor and told him about her plan. He promised to submit her note of interest that same day.

Once she'd hung up, Penny felt simultaneously on high and completely exhausted from dealing with what she considered super-grown-up stuff.

She grabbed a carton of ice cream from the freezer. It was her favorite, black cherry vanilla, and luckily nobody else in the house liked it.

She took it to the garden because she needed to be close to her mother.

On a bench among the rose bushes, she ate her ice cream and told her mom about the cottage.

Suddenly, a rose caught her eye.

She set the carton aside, then pulled the rosebud from the cottage garden out of her jean-jacket pocket.

Carefully plucking petals off, she compared her mother's roses with the specimen from the cottage garden.

It was the exact same kind of rose.

A shiver ran down her spine.

Suddenly, Penny knew the connection was about more than just her.

She felt so sure that she'd found her new home. A place where she belonged.

Everything would be different from now on.

3

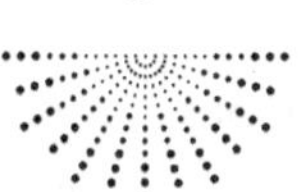

The next morning, Penny's mood was brought down a few notches when Irene called.

"I'm afraid I have some bad news about your offer."

"What?" Penny exclaimed. She was more surprised than anything, since she'd been so sure that this would work out.

"Normally, we wait for all the offers to come in. But in this case, I don't mind telling you, because you could easily deduce it from the home report, that the cottage has been with another agent for years and they never could sell it. I considered it a stroke of luck that you were so interested, and I urged the owners to accept the offer immediately. Instead, the owners decided to up the asking price. Significantly."

"How much higher? I have some savings I was planning to use for the renovations."

Irene named a price almost a third more than what they'd agreed upon yesterday.

Penny's stomach plummeted.

"That's..."

"A lot. I know." Irene sounded annoyed.

"Do you know why the owners reconsidered? Maybe I could talk to them and persuade them they should sell it to me."

Irene exhaled in exasperation. "They wouldn't agree to that. Believe me, I already tried my best to reason with them."

"Like I said, I can pay more, but not that much..." Penny named the amount she could scrape together.

She wouldn't have anything left over for repairs, but she'd worry about that once she owned the cottage.

"Are you sure you want to pay that much? Listen, I have a few other properties I can show you."

"No, it's this cottage. I really need to buy it." Penny couldn't help but sound desperate.

"Hmm. If you don't mind me asking, then—is this personal? Because I got that impression from the owners. That they increased the price so they wouldn't have to sell to you, specifically. I didn't want to say anything, but—"

"What do you mean? Do they know me? What are the owners' names?"

After some hesitation, Irene gave her the information.

"I don't know them," Penny said in desperation. "This must be a mistake."

"No, I don't think so, dear. Penny Reid, daughter of June Reid, right? I didn't know June well, but I met her a couple of times, back when she was still..." Irene cleared her throat. "Anyway, that's you, isn't it?"

"Yes. Strange, if this has to do with my mother. My mother was well liked and didn't have any enemies. If you met her, you understand. I still think this must be a misunderstanding. Please, don't you think I could meet them and talk to them directly?"

"They are adamant. They don't want to talk to you, and they definitely don't want you to buy that property."

"Okay, so what if I manage to get the new asking price together? In cash. Do you think they'd sell it to me, then?"

"I don't know. They clearly don't want to, but I also know they need to sell. That's the reason they switched real estate agents and begged me to take this on. If there aren't any more offers, they may have no choice but to accept yours."

"Okay." The tiniest spark of hope reignited in Penny's chest. "I'll get the money together somehow."

PENNY TRIED to stay positive and hold on to her plan, but she couldn't help but feel down. She found it hard to focus on her work, and her boss reprimanded her several times that day. When Penny knocked a ceramic pot off the shelf, her boss scolded her. "This'll come out of your wages for today! Get out of my sight. Go take care of the seedlings in the greenhouse. You can go straight home from there once your shift is finished. I expect better conduct tomorrow, or you'll get a warning."

Penny was relieved to be sent off to take care of what others might have considered a tedious task. It was hard for her to hold her tongue when her boss spoke to her like that. She would have loved to tell her what she thought of her and couldn't wait to quit this job.

She only stayed because of the decent pay, and she couldn't really afford to lose the job now that her dreams of owning her own rose cottage were almost reachable.

Although...it didn't look as if it'd be easy. Penny was sure the cottage should belong to her. All the signs pointed toward it. What should she do if the owners really refused to sell it to her? Whatever could the reason be?

Penny's thoughts went in circles while she worked as

fast as possible to finish early. She left without saying goodbye to her boss.

Her father was already out "working," but Declan was home. The siblings ate dinner together.

Declan was an earnest and quiet boy, and he rarely told Penny much about his day. But this evening he was bursting with excitement, and he could hardly shut up. During career day at school, Declan had been impressed by a police officer. Now he felt sure he'd found his calling.

Penny felt oddly touched. It took her a moment to name the feeling welling up inside her. There was affection, sure, but something else. Pride.

Suddenly she had doubts about moving out. Yes, their father usually pulled himself together for Declan, but he might lose control at some point. What if Penny wasn't here to defuse a situation or take care of all the little things? What if it all got to be too much for her father and he couldn't look after Declan after all?

How would that affect her little brother's bright future?

Penny wasn't the touchy-feely type, and Declan usually kept his distance too. It was not just the age difference of five years, but an odd dynamic since their father treated them so differently.

But Declan was still her little brother, and Penny felt responsible for him. A part of her wanted to shelter him from harsh reality.

It was enough that one sibling had had a botched start in life because of their parents.

And yes, that evening Penny included her mother. She'd loved and revered her, and on her good days, Penny could be empathetic and mature. But on days like today, bitterness took over. She was a child too. A child who had been abandoned by her mom. Her mom had known that Dad would make her life a living hell since he'd done it to her. Penny knew it wasn't right to blame the victims of abuse. But she still wished that her mother had fought back and not let her father drive her to suicide. She'd needed her mother. Instead of dreaming of and planning her own future, she'd had to take responsibility for her family at age sixteen. It wasn't fair.

After dinner, in her room, Penny wallowed a little in self-pity, but then she made a decision.

She wouldn't repeat her mother's mistakes. She refused to let others ruin her life or be relegated to the role of victim.

She'd find a way to make her dreams come true, come hell or high water.

Financial independence was the path to reaching her goals, that much was clear to her. She needed to earn enough money to buy the cottage and repair it, and then she could get to work in the garden. There, she'd have all the resources she'd need at her fingertips to do something with herbs and plants. Naturally, that's what she was good at, and she'd just need to find a way to make money from her talents. Even though she wasn't sure what to do yet, she was determined to start her own business.

Penny also wanted to hire a housekeeper who could look after the family home and keep an eye on her brother.

She'd need a good chunk of cash to accomplish all that.

Her job at the nursery wouldn't get her very far. But what else could she do?

All she had was a green thumb. Well, that and her beauty.

Many men commented on it, and more than one had tried to buy her with cash or gifts. That, of course, was out of the question. She wouldn't sell her body.

But maybe she could use her good looks to her advantage. It wouldn't be the first time. She usually drew firm lines for herself, but moral scruples wouldn't do her much good in her current situation.

Perhaps she could get a job in sales, somewhere with a chance for big commissions. But what could she sell? Something that was marketed toward men, where her looks and charms would help. Insurance? Cars? She knew nothing about either, and she didn't care to learn.

Sighing, Penny took out the box with all the ingredients she needed for her rituals for the days between the years. Just because nobody had used the cards at other times during the year didn't mean she couldn't.

Maybe they would give her some clue what to do.

She meditated for a long while, then burned some sage and other herbs.

After carefully unwrapping the cards, she spread them out on the low coffee table.

Closing her eyes, she slowly moved her hands over them before picking one and turning it over.

When she opened her eyes and saw the illustration on the card, she got a little jolt.

It was the card with the rose cottage again.

Penny was sure it couldn't be a coincidence. The universe clearly wanted the cottage to be hers. It strengthened Penny's resolve to do whatever she needed to raise the funds to buy it.

Unfortunately, the cards hadn't helped her become any clearer on how to accomplish that. Somewhat frustrated, she started to swipe the cards together when something on the rose cottage card caught her eye.

Certain her eyes were playing a trick on her, she picked the card up.

But she wasn't imagining it. In the background, to the right of the cottage, amid the foliage, was the faint outline of a garden shed.

It was clearly the shed Penny had visited, which she'd dubbed the herb hut.

Penny rubbed the card with her finger, but nothing had been stuck to it. The part with the herb hut didn't look different from the rest of the illustration either.

Everything else looked exactly like she remembered, including the bottles and glasses. But the shed was definitely new. It hadn't been there when she'd picked the card in January. She was one hundred percent sure of it.

If the card hadn't been altered, had it been swapped? But who could have done that? And why? It seemed the only possible logical explanation, but Penny knew it didn't make sense.

In Penny's world, there was another explanation—not a logical one, but a magical one. She belonged to a community of women with supernatural talents and had experienced much stranger things.

She was sure this card was trying to tell her something. It wanted her to pay attention to the herb hut. But she'd already explored it. Would she need to visit it again?

What could she possibly find there?

4

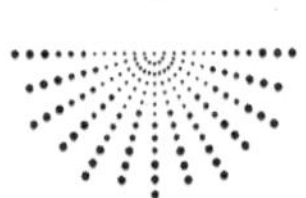

It was already late by the time Penny set off, but this close to the summer solstice, the sky was still fairly light.

Her heart was pounding wildly. Ideas about what she might find in the garden shed were whirling around in her head like a magic lantern.

To her relief, there was nobody at the cottage. The windows were dark, and it looked as uninhabited as last time. There was no vehicle parked in front.

Penny got out of her car and was greeted by the chirping of crickets and the buzzing of insects. This time it was easier to make her way to the back of the house, since she'd already forged a path last time.

Once she was in the garden, she had to stop to catch her breath.

The rose garden was bathed in the pink hues of dusk. The other plants were glowing too. It was almost as if someone had cast a spell over the garden.

Penny followed the path to the herb hut. She took out her flashlight and opened the door.

The beam danced over the table, the Welsh dresser,

and the wooden screen. Penny stepped in to inspect all the corners. All she could see was dust and cobwebs.

She stopped in front of the screen, taking in the illustrations once more, but if they were giving her any clues, she couldn't decipher them.

Next, she turned to the Welsh dresser. There were the jars, glasses, and pestle and mortar on the counter, but she opened the cabinets underneath and looked at the smaller shelves on top.

To her disappointment, it was empty. She even felt around the cupboards, in case there was something hidden, but all she got was a splinter from the old wood.

Sighing, she straightened and looked around one more time, paying attention to the ceiling.

There was a hayloft-style open attic that stretched across half of the shed. Penny assumed it had been used to dry herbs.

There was a rickety ladder leading up to the attic. It didn't look very trustworthy, but Penny dared to step onto it. She needed to see everything in this shed. When she'd climbed up high enough, she stretched up one arm to shine the light around.

Her heart skipped a beat when she discovered the chest in the attic's corner.

Penny scrambled all the way up and carefully moved across the floorboards on all fours, fearing that the wood could be rotten and unable to support her weight.

But she didn't crash through and finally reached the chest.

She opened it eagerly and pointed the light beam inside.

Her eyes widened. She wiped her dirty hand on her T-shirt before taking out some jars and bottles.

Unlike the few she'd seen downstairs, these were full.

She lifted one bottle. It was made of green glass and

was uneven, possibly hand-blown. It contained a dark, viscous liquid. The stopper was sealed with red wax. She examined the bottle closely, but there was no label or inscription.

After a moment's hesitation, Penny removed the wax. Ordinarily, she might have been more cautious, but this bottle looked like one from the card.

The card had sent her here to find it; Penny had no doubt about it.

After another deep breath, Penny pulled out the stopper. It came out slowly, with a lot of effort, but once it had popped, a potent scent emanated from the bottle.

A female voice rang out in the shed. "Spell for unrequited love."

In shock, Penny looked around, shining her flashlight this way and that. But there was nobody besides her inside the herb hut.

The voice was loud, and it echoed from all corners, as if it was all around her.

"Take three handfuls of dark rose petals…"

Penny blinked. Her gaze went to the bottle. Could it be that she had released the voice from the bottle, like a genie?

But there was no apparition, only the voice.

Penny pressed the stopper against the opening of the bottle, and the voice stopped too.

She took the plug off again.

"…grind them with a mortar," the woman's voice in the regional Scottish accent continued.

Penny re-plugged the bottle as best as she could, then eased away from the chest and climbed down the ladder.

She ran out of the hut, through the garden, and back to her car. After yanking open the passenger door, she rummaged around in her glove compartment for a notebook and pen.

Then she returned to the garden shed as fast as she

could. Back in the attic, she put the flashlight on the chest and positioned it so the beam fell across her open notebook. Then she wrote:

Spell for unrequited love

And underneath that she wrote everything else the woman's voice had said, as best as Penny could recall.

Then she picked up the bottle and removed the stopper again.

"Mix the crushed rose petals with three thimbles of evening primrose oil."

Penny scribbled quickly, taking down everything the woman's voice said.

After the directions for the spell had finished, silence reigned in the hut.

Penny waited, pen poised, in case there was more, but nothing came.

Just to be sure, she put the stopper back in, waited a few seconds, and took it out.

Still nothing.

Penny picked up the flashlight to look into the bottle opening. She couldn't see anything but a dark, oily liquid. She held the bottle up to her nose and carefully inhaled. The scent was acrid and unpleasant. There were definitely herbs in this concoction, but something had been done to them, and Penny could no longer identify what they were.

Penny closed the bottle and took some time to think things through.

It was possible that the magic needed recovery time, and once she'd sealed the bottle and let it sit for a long while, the voice might return.

But Penny thought it was more likely that the spoken instructions for the spell had been trapped in the bottle by magic, and once released, they'd be gone forever.

She examined some of the other bottles and jars. Some had stoppers. Others were closed with wire clips, like canning jars. Some were sealed with wax, but others had strips of cloth wrapped around the clip.

Penny opened one container after another, releasing the woman's voice, and wrote down what it said.

After she was done with the last jar, she'd used up all available space in her notebook. She only hoped she could read her hurried scribbles. She definitely needed to write everything down in more legible handwriting as soon as she was home.

Penny put all the empty bottles back into the chest and left the shed.

Adrenaline had filled her as long as she'd been preoccupied with taking down notes from the magic voice, but now exhaustion took over.

Clutching the notebook to her chest, she stumbled back to her car.

"Good bye, rose cottage," she said, before turning the car around to drive home. "See you soon."

Now she had a plan for getting the money needed to buy the cottage.

5

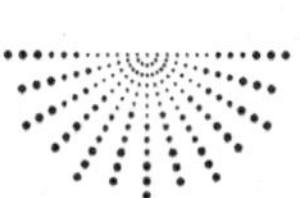

It was the third time Penny had set up her market stall. She was far less enthusiastic today, as she was beginning to doubt her plan.

The spells weren't the problem. She'd followed the instructions and tried out some products. Everything worked perfectly. It was real, powerful herb magic, leagues better than anything her mother had ever taught her. The potions were well worth the money she wanted for them—much more, actually.

The problem was that customers couldn't be convinced to buy them.

They were wary of anything that seemed too good to be true. And they certainly didn't want to buy anything to do with witchcraft, suspecting it to be nothing but mumbo jumbo.

Penny was using her own beauty-spell products to make herself irresistible, so she could persuade men to make some purchases, but she hadn't shifted the big-ticket items and hadn't raised nearly as much money as she'd hoped by now.

There wasn't really any turning back now, though,

because Penny had been so convinced she was on the right path that she'd put all her eggs in one basket.

She'd quit her job at the nursery to have time for her new business, and she'd needed to invest money in ingredients and packaging as well as market-stall fees and other business expenses.

Thanks to some lower-cost beauty products and male customers eager to please her, she was turning a small profit already. Ordinarily, her new business venture would be considered a success.

But time was of the essence. If she didn't get the money together fast enough, somebody else might buy the cottage, and all would be over.

Penny was bone-tired after working so much, and she was frustrated. The only expensive item she'd sold today was a prosperity potion. Ironically, it was one of those spells one couldn't use on oneself.

She felt rather bitter—why had the card sent her down this path if nothing came of it?

Penny was close to packing up her stall and going home when she noticed a woman loitering at the edge.

"Can I help you?" she asked, a little sharply.

The woman seemed startled. She looked around, but nobody else paid them any mind. She scurried over to Penny and whispered, "Do you have love spells?"

Penny's mood lifted. "I do. Several. What exactly are you looking for? I have an anti-break-up spell, a spell to find new love, a potion for unrequited love—"

"That!" the woman shouted, immediately ducking her head and looking around in panic. "That's what I need," she whispered. "How much is it?"

Penny told her the price.

The women's eyes almost popped out of her head. "That's a lot."

"You can't put a high enough price on love," Penny

answered, a little angry. She'd had just about enough. This idea probably wasn't going to work. She sighed. "You know what? I'll make you a special deal if you promise to brag to all of your friends about turning on this man's feelings and tell them where to go if they need something similar. Fifty percent off."

"All right, that doesn't seem too bad." The woman paused. "You seem awfully confident it's going to work."

"Of course it's going to work. I'm the real deal. Tell that to everyone." When the woman still seemed to hesitate, she said, "Look. The bottle is quite full. A few drops will suffice. They need to be ingested. If it doesn't work, you can use the rest as a perfume or to scent a bath. It's basically rose and jasmine, and it smells really nice."

She was close to giving the woman the potion for free, but her arguments seemed to have persuaded her.

"Okay, I'll take it."

"Wonderful." Penny wrapped the bottle up and tied a decorative bow around it. Then she stuck her business card underneath the ribbon. "Here you go. And remember, don't use too much all at once. Only a few drops in the guy's drink."

The woman nodded eagerly. "Thanks."

With another furtive glance around, the woman scurried off.

Penny had an idea. If she wanted to earn enough money for the cottage, she couldn't really give her products away like that. On the other hand, if she didn't sell them, she'd not only fail to accrue the money, she'd also be sitting on a lot of products she couldn't shift.

She gathered a few things to create a makeshift sign.

S*ampling promotion. 50% discount*

The sign didn't exactly create a run on her stand, but she sold much more than before. She tried the same technique at two other markets the following week and at least got rid of a lot of products. So her work hadn't been completely in vain.

The following week, Penny returned to the market in the town where the woman had bought the love potion. She couldn't believe her eyes. There were actually people waiting for her to set up her stall. She barely had time to get ready, and customers were already snatching up the rest of her wares. And this time at full price.

One woman paid a hefty sum for a luck spell, and her companion exclaimed in horror, "Are you crazy to spend that much on such humbug?"

"It's not humbug," the woman answered calmly. "These spells really work. Ruth from Strathyre told me. She's been after this guy for ages, and he'd always rebuffed her advances. Thanks to a love potion from this stall, he's now crazy about her."

The companion still didn't want to believe it, but Penny didn't care. Her customer from last week had kept her promise and had done word-of-mouth marketing.

She hoped Ruth from Strathyre would always be lucky in love.

Penny made a huge profit that day.

Unfortunately, she was out of products and had to put in a lot of work to make enough for the next market. But she didn't mind, now that her plan was finally coming to fruition. Besides, working herb magic was fun, and she was looking forward to it.

Her good mood was dampened, though, when she got home and saw someone waiting for her.

It was Mrs. MacDonald. Officially, she was the chair of the local women's club—which was actually the Tarbet coven.

The old woman looked like a witch, too, with black, unkempt hair, warts on her wrinkled face, and yellow teeth. Her clothes were scruffy and old-fashioned, like she'd worn them ever since she'd ascended to head witch. And nobody could remember when that had been. She had absolute authority, and nobody in the coven dared to dissent.

Penny's face fell when Mrs. MacDonald told her she couldn't carry on with her business.

"You can't publically present yourself as a witch and sell magical products, Penny. That draws too much attention. You'll bring the entire coven into disrepute."

Mrs. MacDonald was so used to the fact that her word was usually the law that she'd already turned around to leave without waiting for Penny's answer.

But there was too much at stake for Penny to give up just like that, coven hierarchy be damned.

"Then I'll leave the coven. You'll have no authority over me, and I can conduct my business however I want."

Clearly surprised, Mrs. MacDonald turned around and regarded Penny searchingly.

"Why is this so important to you? Why are you doing this?"

Penny suddenly realized that Mrs. MacDonald hadn't asked her where she got the spells or how she had suddenly turned into a powerful herb witch.

"Because I really need the money. I want to buy a property, a cottage with a garden, and I think it belongs to me. I almost had enough money, but the owners changed their minds and upped the asking price after they heard I wanted to buy it."

Mrs. MacDonald pursed her lips. "Which cottage?"

Penny told her where the property was located. "I believe that cottage is rightfully mine." She revealed to the coven leader what she had seen in the cards—and how the card had led her to the garden shed, where she'd discovered the spells.

She was ready to argue, but it turned out to be unnecessary.

Mrs. MacDonald agreed with her.

"Yes, you're right. That is your cottage. It once belonged to your grandmother, Lucinda. Her relatives, the current owners, managed to take possession of it, but that wasn't right. Lucinda was born out of wedlock, you see, and back then, that meant she had no legal rights when it came to claiming an inheritance. However, the cottage had belonged to your witch ancestors for generations before that. These relatives forced Lucinda to move out because they wanted the property for themselves, and, like I said, Lucinda had no legal recourse. But rumor has it she cursed the cottage. Since then, the property has brought nothing but misfortune and calamity to those who tried to live there. The owners gave up on it, and nobody dares to buy it, so the cottage has fallen more and more into disrepair."

"I see!" Penny's eyes shone. She finally understood why Irene had been so open about her frustrations with the owners. Finally somebody wanted to buy the cottage, and the owners were throwing a spanner in the works.

And Mrs. MacDonald also confirmed what she had felt in her gut all this time. The cottage really belonged to her. It had been in her family. The card had led her to find it and reclaim it.

"The real estate agent was right, then. This is personal. The owners don't want to sell it to me because I'm a descendant of Lucinda's. But according to the agent, they can't hold out much longer. They need the money. If I were to pay the ridiculously high asking price, she thinks they'd eventually swallow their pride and agree to the sale."

Mrs. MacDonald thought about it for a while, then she said, "I understand why you're doing everything you can to earn enough money to buy the cottage. I think you should buy it. And I see that this is the only way. But I can't let you draw this much attention to your herbal magic. If you'd do it more covertly and to help people, instead of putting financial gain first—"

"I can't. It's too slow. I need the money soon!"

Mrs. MacDonald shook her head. "It simply won't do. You're risking everything. And you're putting the coven at risk. But I can help you. We'll do this another way."

"How?" Penny couldn't help but sound exasperated.

Mrs. MacDonald furrowed her already wrinkly brow. "If I remember correctly, your mother left you an inheritance?"

"Yes. That's what I earmarked for purchasing my own place as soon as I was able to. It would have worked out, too, because the original asking price was pretty much the same amount. But now…" She raked her fingers through her blond locks.

"Are you sure you know what the amount was? When was the last time you checked?"

"What do you mean? I haven't check since the solicitor told us about the trust. But it'll be roughly the same. It wouldn't have accrued much interest. My father always wanted it to be paid out to him, because I was a minor, but I told the solicitor I didn't want that, and he agreed the will stipulated that it was mine. You don't think my dad managed to get his hands on some of the money, or…"

Penny stopped talking because there was a funny expression in Mrs. MacDonald's eyes.

"Hmmm. Why don't you check? Maybe you'll find that you didn't remember the right amount after all—or that it did accrue more interest." Mrs. MacDonald winked at her.

Penny shook her head in confusion. It sounded as if Mrs. MacDonald expected the amount to be more than she'd been informed about at age fourteen, but she didn't see how that could be possible.

"Just go to the bank tomorrow, Penny. I'm sure it'll sort itself out. You might be in for a pleasant surprise."

Mrs. MacDonald left, and Penny could only stare after her.

If she hadn't known better, she'd figure the old woman had lost her marbles.

But this was her coven leader, and she *knew* things. In any case, Penny was desperate. It wouldn't hurt to double-check on her financial situation.

6

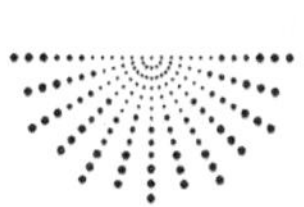

Just to have all her bases covered, Penny kept herself busy making new products that evening and the following morning.

After lunch, she set off for to the bank in Helensburgh. During her phone conversation with the solicitor about the offer for the cottage, she'd already confirmed her access to the money. "It became yours to access the moment you turned eighteen," he'd told her and given her the bank details.

Now, at the bank counter, Penny showed her identification and asked for the current balance.

"I put in an offer for a house," she told the bank clerk. "And I need the money for that."

The woman looked her up and down. "Aren't you a bit young to buy a house?"

Penny just held her chin up. "Just let me know the amount. I've been told my inheritance money might have accrued some interest since I last checked."

The bank clerk made a show of double-checking the ID and the account paperwork. Her demeanor changed when she looked at the computer screen, though. "Oh my.

Looks like you have the means to buy a house after all, Miss Reid." She read out the numbers on the screen.

Penny just stared at her.

Mrs. MacDonald had been right. She had the money for the much higher asking price. She'd been a hundred percent sure of what her mother had left her. It had been a number in her head that, in the last four years, had served as a life raft. It had meant that one day she'd get out of her dad's house and be independent.

So Penny was sure she hadn't misremembered. Somehow, Mrs. MacDonald must have worked magic to make the sum bigger.

"Are you all right, miss?" the bank clerk said.

"Um, yes. I'm okay. I'm just thinking. Obviously, I've never done this before." She gave a demure smile. "How does it work if I want to buy this house outright? Do we transfer the money into my checking account, or..."

The bank clerk's expression softened. In a motherly tone, she said, "Of course you don't know, dear. We can help you. Why don't you go into the office and I'll get Mr. Mullins, my superior, to talk everything through with you?"

"Thank you," Penny said with relief.

The bank clerk showed her into the office. "Do you want a coffee? Or juice?"

"Just water would be great, thanks." Penny's throat was quite parched.

"I'll get you some. And I'll also let Mr. Mullins know you're in here."

"Great! Actually," Penny said, "do you mind if I make a quick phone call?"

"Go right ahead, dear." The clerk pointed at the phone on the desk.

Penny dug the piece of paper with the real estate agent's phone number out of her bag, then dialed the number.

"Irene? This is Penny Reid. I've got the money. And I'm at the bank right now. I can buy the cottage outright. In cash."

Irene was taken aback. "Are you sure you want to spend that much money on a dilapidated cottage? Like I've said, I could show you some lovely properties, and if you have the means—"

"No, it has to be this property. Do you think the owners will sell it to me for this price, even though they don't want to?"

"To be honest, they'd be foolish not to. I happen to know they need the money. I'll call them right away."

"Okay, great. I'm at the bank right now. Call me back at this number if you can talk to them and convince them in the next half hour." She read the number off the phone.

"Will do. Speak to you soon."

Just as Penny was hanging up, Mr. Mullins came in.

"Miss Reid, what can I do for you?" The bank manager shook Penny's hand.

Penny explained the situation to him, and the bank manager walked her through how they would wire the money and then close the account.

When they'd discussed everything, the phone rang. "That might be my real estate agent," Penny said nervously.

Mr. Mullins picked up. "Oh, Irene, it's you."

Clearly they knew each other, most likely having had dealings before, and they engaged in some chitchat.

Penny could hardly stay in her seat. She was close to ripping the receiver out of the bank manager's hand when he finally handed it to her.

"Good news," Irene said. "When they heard how much you're willing to pay, they needed little convincing to agree to the sale."

Penny was so relieved, she only half listened when

Irene hinted at the fact that her relatives saw it as having gotten one over on her—and, by extension, her grandmother. Some form of comeuppance after they'd suffered from Lucinda's curse for all those years. Penny didn't know these people, and she didn't care to. All she cared about was the cottage. "Oh my god, that's such good news."

"Listen, I know Mr. Mullins, so if you pass the phone back to him, I'll sort out everything we need to ascertain your ability to pay in cash, like you wanted. You can come to my office tomorrow, say at nine? I'll draw up the paperwork by then. Don't forget to inform your solicitor too."

Penny agreed, thanked the bank manager, and said goodbye so he could talk with Irene.

She was a little numb when she left the bank, smiling weakly at the bank clerk.

Penny didn't understand what had happened, and she couldn't celebrate just yet.

Even if everything held up until the next day, when she'd sign the paperwork, house purchases didn't happen overnight.

What if Mrs. MacDonald had only fixed this with a temporary spell? Surely she couldn't have actually magicked money that hadn't been there in the first place. What if the sizable sum in her bank account was nothing but a mirage?

What if tomorrow, or in the coming month, it turned out that she didn't have the money after all, and the deal fell through?

No, she couldn't live with the worry hanging over her.

Instead of driving home, Penny went to Mrs. MacDonald's house.

When the older woman opened the door, Penny wasn't sure if she should hug her—but then neither she nor the coven leader were prone to showing their affection that way.

So she just grabbed Mrs. MacDonald's hand. "Thank you, thank you, thank you," she said.

"Come in," was the dry response.

Penny followed Mrs. MacDonald into the kitchen.

"How on earth did you do it?" she asked before she'd even taken a seat. "You didn't use your own..." Penny stopped when she took in Mrs. MacDonald's old-fashioned and dirty kitchen. No, it was impossible. The coven leader didn't have that kind of money.

"You're a member of our coven. The cottage is your rightful heritage. I think it's important for you, so you can become the witch you're supposed to be. As your coven leader, it was my job to help you. I can't give you the details, but rest assured, the amount of your mother's inheritance has always been the one you've been told today. So you don't need to worry someone will find out the account has been tampered with or anything. That didn't happen. It won't somehow turn back to the amount you remembered because that amount never existed."

Penny was stumped and really didn't know what to make of the explanation.

Mrs. MacDonald, who had been preparing a pot of tea as she was answering, now turned around. "But Penny, promise me you'll stop selling your potions and spells so publicly. We don't need that attention—and you don't want that reputation either."

Some of Penny's elation immediately evaporated. She was very grateful to Mrs. MacDonald for helping her—and as a result, she couldn't really turn down her request.

Well played, Mrs. M., Penny thought. With a petulant note in her voice, she said, "But I quit my job at the nursery. I have to keep my business. How else am I going to pay for the repairs? I still need to make a living, and I really need to hire a housekeeper for Declan and my father."

"You can keep your business and make all sorts of non-magical products with herbs and plants."

Penny crossed her arms in front of her chest. "You can't ask me to leave magic out of it. Herbal witchcraft is part of my identity. I'm only now discovering more about it. And I think I'm supposed to *own it*, you know? That's why I was set on the path to discovering the cottage and the instructions my grandmother left for me. You don't want me to ignore it and let this knowledge go to waste, do you?"

She held her breath, waiting for Mrs. MacDonald's response. Would the wrath of the coven leader rain down on her?

But Mrs. MacDonald just rolled her eyes. "By all means, use magic. Just don't advertise it as such. You're young. You need to experiment and make your own mistakes. If in doubt or if something gets out of control, come to us. Do we understand each other?"

Now it was Penny's turn to roll her eyes. "All right," she conceded. She didn't really have a choice. And it really wasn't too bad. She'd still make money, just not as much. And really, Mrs. MacDonald had only asked her to be discreet, hadn't she?

She could make it work.

~

August 1996

PENNY SAT on the stone bench in the middle of her rose garden and opened a bottle of champagne. She'd finally moved into her cottage. The house, the garden, and the herb hut were now officially her new home.

She didn't have a champagne flute—in fact, she didn't own any glasses yet, but she'd purchased beautiful ceramic mugs from a market stall earlier this week. She was on her own, and she didn't have to worry about what anyone thought if she drank champagne out of earthenware.

Before she'd even taken her first celebratory sip, Penny was already drunk—on independence.

It was the best feeling in the world.

She didn't even secretly wish that she could share the moment with anyone. One day, far in the future, she might like a partner, someone to share her home and these moments with.

But letting someone into your life always came with responsibilities. Penny might be young—a fact that everyone seemed so keen to impress upon her—but she had already wised up on one thing: Love came with strings attached, and the worst thing was that in the beginning, when you saw everything through rose-tinted glasses, you couldn't perceive the strings.

Penny didn't want any of that. She wanted to be free and do her own thing.

She'd still be part of the coven, though, so it wasn't as if she was a completely free agent. But she could live with that.

Penny lifted her cup to the roses—and that's when she remembered she wasn't actually alone after all.

There was someone here, at least in spirit, and she didn't mind sharing this place—or this celebration—with this person.

They were as much hers as they were Penny's.

Penny stood up and looked toward the herb hut. Some of the roof and a wall were barely visible from where she was standing.

She raised her mug.

"Thank you, and cheers, Grandma Lucinda."

Thank you for reading WITCHY MUSE AND GHOSTLY CLUES and HEX MARKS THE COTTAGE. I hope you enjoyed reading them as much as I loved writing them. If you did, I would greatly appreciate a review on Amazon or your favorite store or book review site. Reviews are crucial for authors as well as for readers who are looking for their next book—even just a line or two are so helpful. Thanks!

I love to chat with my readers, so if you'd like to contact me, visit felicitygreenauthor.com.

Are you excited for another SCOTTISH WITCHES installment? Sign up for my newsletter on felicitygreenauthor.com, so you won't miss information on new releases. You'll also receive a free book, NO REST FOR THE WICKED WITCH.

Happy reading!

Felicity Green

www.ingramcontent.com/pod-product-compliance
Lightning Source LLC
LaVergne TN
LVHW091409190726
843491LV00006B/1337

* 9 7 8 3 9 1 1 2 3 8 0 6 9 *